Ready, Willing, and Stable

Longarm studied the stable wall. "These boards are barely hanging on to their warped studs. I say we kick 'em in and dive through the wall with our guns at the ready."

He and Barstow reared back and kicked the boards, which offered no more resistance than expected. With a sudden hole in the barn, the two lawmen dove through the new opening with their guns up and ready to fire.

The deafening blast of a shotgun was followed by twin flashes that lit up the dark interior of the big stable. Longarm felt the sting of a shot slash across his forearm, and he instinctively fired.

They heard a yelp and then a curse, followed by the sound of hard-running feet.

"He's getting away!" Barstow shouted. "Go after him!"

Longarm was already up and moving, and was damned unhappy about the prospect of a long chase.

He then caught a glimpse of the man disappearing into an alley. Longarm immediately realized it was a dead end bordered by dirty brick buildings. There was no way out—but there was a hellish mix of swarming mosquitoes and biting horseflies gorging on garbage.

It was a bad place to fight—and an even worse place to die . . .

TABOR EVANS

LONGARM

AND THE GILA RIVER MURDERS

JOVE BOOKS, NEW YORK

THE BERKLEY PUBLISHING GROUP
Published by the Penguin Group
Penguin Group (USA) Inc.
375 Hudson Street, New York, New York 10014, USA
Penguin Group (Canada), 90 Eglinton Avenue East, Suite 700, Toronto, Ontario M4P 2Y3, Canada
(a division of Pearson Penguin Canada Inc.)
Penguin Books Ltd., 80 Strand, London WC2R 0RL, England
Penguin Group Ireland, 25 St. Stephen's Green, Dublin 2, Ireland (a division of Penguin Books Ltd.)
Penguin Group (Australia), 250 Camberwell Road, Camberwell, Victoria 3124, Australia
(a division of Pearson Australia Group Pty. Ltd.)
Penguin Books India Pvt. Ltd., 11 Community Centre, Panchsheel Park, New Delhi—110 017, India
Penguin Group (NZ), 67 Apollo Drive, Rosedale, North Shore 0632, New Zealand
(a division of Pearson New Zealand Ltd.)
Penguin Books (South Africa) (Pty.) Ltd., 24 Sturdee Avenue, Rosebank, Johannesburg 2196,
South Africa

Penguin Books Ltd., Registered Offices: 80 Strand, London WC2R 0RL, England

This is a work of fiction. Names, characters, places, and incidents either are the product of the author's imagination or are used fictitiously, and any resemblance to actual persons, living or dead, business establishments, events, or locales is entirely coincidental.

LONGARM AND THE GILA RIVER MURDERS

A Jove Book / published by arrangement with the author

PRINTING HISTORY
Jove edition / August 2009

Copyright © 2009 by Penguin Group (USA) Inc.
Cover illustration by Miro Sinovcic.

ISBN: 978-0-515-14663-9

JOVE®
Jove Books are published by The Berkley Publishing Group,
a division of Penguin Group (USA) Inc.,
375 Hudson Street, New York, New York 10014.
JOVE® is a registered trademark of Penguin Group (USA) Inc.
The "J" design is a trademark of Penguin Group (USA) Inc.

PRINTED IN THE UNITED STATES OF AMERICA

10 9 8 7 6 5 4 3 2 1

Chapter 1

Deputy United States Marshal Custis Long was feeling very good about himself this brisk April morning as he strolled past the Denver Mint on his way to his office at the Federal Building. It was one of those breezy, cloudless spring days when the world seemed more alive and vibrant than usual, and he was humming a tune. Today was Friday and Longarm had a date with a very special brunette that evening. But suddenly, he heard a gunshot just a block up the street, and then a large, wild-eyed man with a face full of red beard burst from the crowd and sprinted directly toward Longarm waving a gun and shouting curses. Longarm was a man of action, and he reacted instinctively by drawing his own pistol and coolly stepping behind a lamppost to give himself a little protection and to steady his own aim.

"Halt!" he shouted. "Drop that gun!"

But the big man had no intention of giving himself up on crowded Colfax Avenue, and instead raised his pistol and fired at Longarm. Considering the man was running hard, his bullet was amazingly well aimed and clipped Longarm's snuff brown hat with its flat brim. That same bullet then struck a young woman in the arm, spinning her completely around. With a cry of pain, she fell into the street right in front of an oncoming freight wagon. Longarm had an instant of indecision. He was the only person close enough and quick enough to save the woman from being run over and almost certainly killed, but the man with the gun was bearing down on him and firing in his direction.

Longarm snapped off a shot that struck the big man in the shoulder, and then the lawman spun around and lunged to help the fallen woman. Being a tall, strong man, Longarm was able to grab her and yank her out of the path of the freight wagon a split second before she would have been crushed by the huge iron wheels.

Dazed and already in shock from the bullet wound, the woman tried to pull away from Longarm.

"Stay still," the deputy marshal ordered, twisting around and taking aim at the big man, who had passed him by and was racing wildly down the sidewalk. Longarm had never been one to put a bullet in someone's back, but right now he felt that it was justified. However, just as he was about to squeeze off a shot, a panicked pedestrian darted into his line of fire.

"Damn!" Longarm cursed as he eased his finger off the trigger and watched the crazy big man with the wild red beard disappear into the crowd. "Dammit anyway!"

Longarm turned his attention back to the young woman, who had just fainted at his side. He could see blood welling up from the bullet hole in her upper right arm. She was bleeding badly, and he removed his clean handkerchief and tied it over the wound to staunch the flow of blood.

By now, the usual morning crowd of mostly office workers had gathered around, and they were chattering and shouting unhelpful advice. Longarm finished tying the handkerchief and said, "Does anyone know who this young woman is? Her name? Where she works?"

"I know her," an older man offered, eagerly stepping forward. "That's Miss Cindy Allison and she works at the United States Mint. She's a nice young lady and . . ."

"Go to the Mint and inform her boss what happened," Longarm interrupted. "Find out where this woman lives and if she has any family."

"I'm quite sure that she lives alone," the man said, his voice decisive. "I work on the same floor as Miss Allison does, and all she has is a cat that she adores. I think she's a ranch girl from down near Tucson, Arizona."

"No family here in Denver?"

"I'm afraid not."

"She's not critically wounded, but she needs a doctor's immediate attention," Longarm said, scooping up Cindy Allison, who was pale and trembling. "The nearest doctor's office is just a block up the street here on Colfax Avenue. I'll take her there, and you make sure that her boss gets in touch with anyone who can care for her."

"What's the doctor's name?" the older man called as Longarm hurried up the street.

"Hell if I know!" Longarm shouted over his shoulder. He was going to add something when he heard three more gunshots that sounded as if they originated a block or two up Colfax. It was almost certainly the crazy red-bearded maniac, and the gunshots made Longarm swear in helplessness. "Damn!"

Longarm hoped that these last three gunshots were the result of a Denver policeman shooting the wild man. But he had a feeling that they were not. More likely, someone else that was completely innocent had just been shot and either killed or wounded by the deranged giant.

I know what he looks like. I put a bullet in his left shoulder. I'll hunt him down and either arrest or kill him myself if he has gotten away, Longarm told himself as he glanced down at the pretty young woman that he carried up the street. She had blond hair, and he remembered that she had blue eyes. There were freckles on her cheeks and although she was not especially tall, she was solid and he could feel that she was surprisingly muscular for a woman. Miss Cindy Allison was not a city-raised hothouse flower. Nope. Longarm understood that she was an Arizona rancher's daughter who had obviously spent almost all of her life doing hard manual labor.

"Clear a way!" Longarm yelled at the curious crowd on Colfax. "Clear a way 'cause I'm comin' through!"

The crowd parted, and Longarm hurried as fast as he could up the sidewalk toward the doctor's office. But when he reached the door, there was a sign telling him that the doctor would not be back in his office until at least ten o'clock that morning.

Longarm swore under his breath and bent his head to decide on his next move. The young woman was still unconscious, and although he had done his absolute best to staunch the bleeding from her arm, it was dripping steadily and she was losing a considerable amount of blood.

"Where is the nearest doctor's office!" he shouted at the people who stood and stared at him and the wounded woman.

"You're standing in front of it," a man replied.

"I know that, you idiot! But this office is closed! The doctor is out until ten o'clock."

"But I just saw the doctor enter that office a few minutes ago."

Longarm reached out and tore the sign off the door, yelling, "Open it up for me!" at the man.

"It's . . . it's locked!"

Longarm lost his temper. Balancing himself on one foot, he reared back with the other and kicked the door so hard that it slammed open splintering wood. "Is there a doctor here!" he yelled, bursting into the empty front office.

A small, bald man in a black suit with a starched shirt and collar stuck his head around a corner and cried. "My God, man! I'm the doctor, but you don't need to destroy the door!"

"I wouldn't have if you'd have been thoughtful enough to remove that sign. I've got a wounded girl here. Move it, Doc!"

The smallish doctor started to snap at Longarm, and then saw the steady drops of blood that were ruining his carpet. "Get her in here on the table," he ordered. "What the hell happened to her?"

"She's been shot. Didn't you hear the gunfire outside?"

"No," the doctor said. "I was in the war and my hearing is faulty due to cannon fire on the lines."

"Well," Longarm said, hurrying into the examination room and gently setting the girl down on the table, "I hope that your medical skills are better than your hearing."

"I was a surgeon in the Union Army."

"Then you know how to remove bullets," Longarm said. "Get it done and get that bleeding stopped."

"How dare you tell me how to practice medicine!"

Longarm grabbed the bald physician by his lapels and shook him like a terrier would a rat. "What the hell is the matter with you!" he yelled in the smaller man's face. "Instead of talking, you ought to be acting to stop the bleeding."

Up close and face-to-face, Longarm was hit hard by the doctor's foul whiskey breath. "Are you drunk!"

"Only half drunk," the man cried. "That's why I didn't take down the sign in the door. I wanted an hour or two to sober up completely before I started seeing patients."

"Well, you haven't got an hour or two. And if you don't act professionally and take care of Miss Allison, you're going to need a doctor to take care of your own damn injuries! I'm a United States marshal and I hope for your sake that I'm making myself clear."

The doctor nodded his head vigorously. "Stand back and let me examine that wound, Marshal."

"I've a hunch that the bullet is still in her arm, but I didn't want to take the time to find out for certain," Longarm said.

The doctor unwrapped Longarm's bloody handkerchief and quickly examined the arm. "There is no exit wound. You're right. The bullet is still in her arm."

"Get it out and get that bullet hole closed up, Doc."

The doctor looked unhealthy and shaken. "Marshal, why don't you step out into the front waiting room?"

"To hell with that. You're half drunk and I'm going to stay right here and make sure you don't mess this up."

"It's only an arm wound! I've dug bullets out of bellies, for cripes sakes! Now get out of here."

"No," Longarm told the man. He stepped back and folded his arms across his chest. "If you somehow allow this young lady to bleed to death on your examination table, then I promise you that I will arrest you for murder and malpractice."

The doctor swallowed hard and looked like he wanted to vomit. Instead, he rushed across the room to a cabinet where he kept his surgical kit. Spilling instruments on the floor in his haste, he managed to find what he was seeking, and then he wasted no time in inserting the long-nosed forceps into the wound. He was sweating profusely and his hand shook, but he closed his eyes and a moment later, he had the slug out and was washing the wound out with antiseptic. "It's a nasty wound and it will leave a scar, but it didn't strike bone or tear anything important to shreds."

He took her pulse and used a stethoscope to listen to her heartbeat. "This young lady is strong. She's going to be all right, Marshal. So why don't you go out into the waiting room?"

"Not a chance," Longarm said. "Sew and bandage it up," he ordered. "I've seen too many doctors that were drunk make bad mistakes."

"I'm not drunk!" the man cried. "I'm just . . . just a little hungover. I'm fine."

"I don't give a damn about you," Longarm said. "It's the girl that I'm worried about."

"Can she pay for my services?"

It was all Longarm could do to contain his fury and not beat this physician into unconsciousness. But he did manage to restrain himself from attacking, and the sweaty, balding little doctor did clean, stitch, and bandage the wound up properly.

"Who takes responsibility for her and my fee?" the doctor asked when he was finished. He licked his lips and mopped his brow dry. "I can't work for free, you know. I've got bills to pay like everyone else."

"I'll pay," Longarm said.

"Glad to hear it, Marshal. That will be five dollars in cash."

Longarm threw the five dollars at the man's feet. Then he picked up the girl and started for the street.

"Where are you taking her?"

"Anywhere but here, Doc," Longarm said, kicking the door the rest of the way off its hinges on his way out.

"Hey! That will cost you another five dollars to replace my door!"

Longarm didn't even bother to reply. The doctor didn't realize it, but if it hadn't been for the still-unconscious ranch girl in Longarm's arms, he would have gotten one hell of a thrashing.

Chapter 2

"Who . . . who are you!" Miss Cindy Allison moaned, after opening her eyes and looking around. "And what . . . where is that crazy man that was trying to kill me?"

"Actually," Longarm said, "I believe that I was his target, not you."

"Where am I?"

Longarm gave her his best and most reassuring smile. "I didn't know where you lived, so after we left the doctor's office, I brought you here to my place."

"I should be at work!" She tried to jump off Longarm's old horsehair couch that had seen much better days, but he gently restrained her and said, "Just take it easy, Miss Allison. I sent word to your boss at the Mint and now they know you were wounded."

"But . . . but I don't understand any of this."

"There was some fella down on Colfax that knew you and where you worked," Longarm explained. "I told him to go and tell your boss about the shooting and how you were an innocent bystander who was wounded by some crazy man in the street. Or maybe he wasn't crazy."

"What do you mean?"

Longarm shrugged. "I have sent a lot of men to the gallows and to prison. So I've got plenty of enemies. Men who would like nothing better than to give me some payback."

"Was that man one of them?"

"I didn't recognize him," Longarm answered. "And I'm sure that I would have remembered a huge, red-bearded man with crazy eyes. But he might have been a relative of someone that wanted to get even with me."

Cindy's blue eyes dropped to the bandage on her upper arm. Her eyes widened with concern. "A bullet wound?"

"Yes, but you're going to be all right," Longarm said, quickly reassuring the young woman. "You lost quite a bit of blood, but the doctor sewed you up and announced that you would heal just fine."

"I don't even remember a doctor."

"He was barely competent."

"And who are you?"

Longarm eased back his coat to display his marshal's badge. "Marshal Custis Long and I'm completely at your service."

Cindy shook her head in wonder. "Now I remember you. Just for an instant, though. You jumped behind a lamppost and I remember you taking aim at the man that was shooting. That huge lunatic with the red beard. Did you kill him, Marshal?"

"I'm afraid not, but I put a slug high up in his shoulder. After we figure out where you live and get you there, I'm going to have to file a report on the shooting. I heard more gunshots and I'm afraid that you might not have been the only innocent bystander to be either wounded or killed this morning."

Cindy shuddered and her eyes took on a faraway look. "Marshal, I seem to recall falling in the street, and there was this big freight wagon and. . . . I guess I blacked out."

"You were nearly run over," Longarm told her. "But I was fortunate enough to be able to grab and pull you out of danger before that happened."

Cindy pushed back her blond hair and sat up slowly. "I feel a little weak and dizzy."

"Miss Allison, as I said earlier, you lost quite a bit of blood."

"I did?"

"Yes. You need to rest for a few days."

"Oh, that may be true, but I need to work and earn money."

"Today is Friday," he explained. "You wouldn't work on Saturday or Sunday anyway at the Mint."

"I work there full-time and work part-time at another job. I really need the money."

"You need the rest more," he said. "Trust me, Miss Allison. When someone has lost as much blood as you did, they need to recuperate at least for a few days. Otherwise, you could pass out on your feet and take a nasty spill. You might even land in a way that breaks open those stitches and the wound would start bleeding again."

She sighed with exasperation. "Well, this is one hell of a sorry situation. Excuse my language, Marshal, but I really need to work tomorrow."

"Are you in that much financial difficulty?"

"Not me. My family. You see, I'm a rancher's daughter from Arizona and my father suffered a mild stroke that left him paralyzed in one arm. On top of that, my mother got pneumonia this past winter and we had a mountain of doctor bills to pay between the two medical emergencies. And then the cattle market went to hell in a handbasket, and on top of everything, my kid brother tried to rob a supply store in Yuma. He's only sixteen and figured we were so desperate for cash that he'd take a chance. The chance didn't pay off and he went before a judge who was inclined to send him to the territorial prison in Yuma."

"I've seen that hellhole a few times too often," Longarm told her. "A sixteen-year-old kid wouldn't last long in that kind of a place. The heat and the suffering there are as bad as it gets in any prison."

"I know," Cindy replied. "It would have been my kid brother's death sentence. So we sold most of our cattle to pay the best lawyer we could find in Yuma. We got Monty off on probation, and even managed to pay the lion's share of the medical bills . . . but there was nothing left for my family to live on. And just as bad, we had no livestock to build back our herd."

"Southern Arizona is pretty hot, dry country for cattle ranching," Longarm said with a sympathetic smile. "I'd think it better suited for raising scorpions, lizards, Gila monsters, and rattlesnakes than cattle."

"Oh, you're certainly right about that. But my family

owns a ranch located along the Gila River that is not far
from the Colorado River. We've always managed to
divert enough water from the Gila River into our fields
to grow feed for our livestock. And my father owns a
small steamboat, and he supplements our income by
hauling supplies up the Colorado for the United States
Army. Between the two things, we always managed to
get by, and in some of the better years, we actually pros-
pered. But with all the misfortune we've had lately, I'm
afraid . . ."

Her words trailed off and her eyes grew distant and
misty.

"Afraid of what?" Longarm finally asked.

"I'm afraid that we've gone into debt so much that
we'll never get back on our feet. There are people who
want to buy our land, Marshal. But when they smell
blood, what they really want to do is to *steal* it."

Cindy shook her head and her mouth formed a hard
line. "They call themselves land speculators. Bankers.
Real estate wheelers and dealers. But in truth, they're
nothing but filthy turkey vultures. And so they flock
around our ranch and caw up their ridiculously low offers. So far, my parents have held them off, but I don't
know how much longer they can keep the vultures at
bay."

"So why aren't you on the ranch giving them all your
support instead of living here in Denver and working at
the United States Mint?"

"I had a friend in Yuma," she said. "He came to
Denver and did very well for himself. He was twelve
years older than me, but I could tell he had a strong attraction for me even when I was just a girl on a pony.

After a few years of being gone, he returned and tried to court me, but I'd have none of that, and my folks didn't much like him even if he had made good in the big city. He left, and then began to write me every week. Some of his letters were . . . well, pretty passionate and I never showed them to my parents."

"What is his name?"

She didn't seem to hear Longarm's question, and continued. "He promised that he could help me get a job with the federal government. He said that he had risen up and was a bigwig at the Mint here, and he could hire whoever he wanted to hire with no questions asked."

"But there were strings," Longarm said, pretty sure that he knew exactly where Miss Allison's story was headed.

"Of course," she admitted. "I was just a hardworking ranch girl. I was well taught by my mother and excellent at arithmetic and spelling, but I'd never even been to a big city, and I knew that I'd be lost without a friend to help me get settled. I knew that, without a friend in the city, I would fall into very bad circumstances. I'd heard the stories of country girls like myself and what they wound up doing in towns."

"So you left your Arizona ranch on the Gila River and came to Denver and hooked up with your so-called friend."

"I did," she confessed. "For the life of me, I just couldn't think of any other way to help my parents keep our ranch. Bradley promised me a very good wage. He said he would find me a cheap apartment all my own and I'd be safe. I'd be making more money in one month than I could have made in three breaking colts or working on a Colorado River barge. Or cooking for cowboys on some ranch or at the Yuma Prison."

"But Bradley," Longarm said, "sure wasn't doing you a favor out of the goodness of his lecherous heart."

"No," she said, lowering her eyes. "He definitely was not."

"You don't have to say anything more."

"I know," she told him. "But I've started my story and I might as well finish. Bradley, you see, is a high-ranking official at the Denver Mint, and he got me through the door just as he'd promised in all those love letters I hid from my folks. Only trouble is, in return, I had to go through his bedroom door."

Longarm glanced away for a moment. "You could have gone to work other places."

"Not really. Bradley knew that I was a ranch girl and had no office skills. He put me to work in his own office filing papers. After a few weeks of working real hard, I was given more important tasks. I realized that I had some brains and a real knack with numbers. At the end of only two months, I was in accounting and carrying my own weight. When someone even higher up than Bradley asked me to work in his office . . . with no bedroom strings attached . . . I jumped at the opportunity."

"So you got rid of Bradley and . . ."

"Not exactly," she said, unable to hide the bitterness in her voice. "Bradley didn't appreciate my getting promoted out from under his thumb. He called me aside one day in private and told me that he would smear my reputation if I didn't come back to work for him. But I refused."

"And then?"

"Then Bradley vowed to tell everyone at the Mint that I was a . . . a whore."

Longarm's big fists clenched at his sides. "So he out and out blackmailed you."

"Yes," Cindy confessed. "He did. I knew that I'd get fired if he started to tell everyone that I came to Denver with nothing but what I had between my legs in exchange for a government job. And Bradley even did it one better with his threat."

Longarm blinked. "What do you mean?"

"He threatened to write my parents a letter telling them about how good I was in his bed. How . . ."

Cindy couldn't finish. Tears filled her eyes and she looked away. "I just couldn't bear the idea of my parents learning what I was willing to do to get a government job. They've had so much grief and heartache from my younger brother that I'm afraid that they've put me on a pedestal. If they'd learned I was Bradley's sex slave . . . why, it would have killed them, and that in turn would have killed me."

Longarm's expression grew hard. "This Bradley fella. He still work at the Mint?"

"Of course. Why do you want to know?"

"I have friends in high places. A few of them at the Mint."

"No, you can't get involved."

"Why not?"

"Well, for one thing, I'd be immediately fired. And for another, Bradley keeps his things at my apartment and he comes over pretty often."

Longarm's eyebrows arched. "Do say."

"Yes."

"And when he does, he just reels you right into the bedroom and tells you to do what pleases him most?"

She swallowed hard and nodded, looking ashamed of herself.

"This guy is a real bastard," Longarm declared in anger. "He needs to be taught some lessons in how to treat a lady."

"I'm not a lady and I'll handle this on my own somehow. I just need to keep my job for a while longer. If I can come up with a few more months of savings, then maybe I can quit or find some other employment. Maybe you even know of a job in accounting where you work."

Longarm had to chuckle at that. "Maybe I do and maybe I don't. But I will ask around. I'm not worth a damn at numbers myself, but people like you seem to have no trouble finding good jobs at banks and other government offices."

Hope sprang into Cindy's eyes. "Oh, I would be so happy if I could just get away from Bradley and his constant demands. But please don't muddy the waters at the Mint for me."

"All right," Longarm promised. "What you do is your own business. But it sure galls me to think that some high-ranking asshole at the Mint is using you the way he is right now."

"Marshal, to be entirely candid, I wasn't a blushing virgin when I came to Denver," she said in a low voice. "I'm a twenty-four-year-old woman and I've seen the best and the worst of what life has to offer. I've known riverboat men and I've known a few handsome cowboys. Some of them were almost as tall and handsome as you, but most weren't. Some were smooth talkers, and one cute boy whose parents owned a ranch not far from ours actually stuttered when he was around me, but he was very nice and maybe the best one of the bunch that came courting. What I'm trying to say is that I wasn't blind about what I was getting into when I agreed to come to Denver and work for Bradley."

"Do you really think that being under Bradley's thumb and going down for him whenever he wants is worth the sacrifice you have to pay?"

"It is for me right now," she answered, her chin lifting. "But when I quit and have enough money to put my family back on its feet and buy us a foundation herd of cattle, I'm going to settle the score with Bradley."

Longarm had to smile at that vow. He liked strong women and had no use for weak ones. He really appreciated and respected women who might be abused once in a while by a man, but who would in the end get their just revenge and walk away with their heads held high. Most frontier women he knew just took the abuse as if it were their due . . . but not all of 'em. And for certain, not this one from Arizona.

Longarm leaned in a little closer. "You gonna tell me what you have in mind for Bradley?"

"No," she said. "I've already said far too much. I shouldn't have unburdened myself on you, Marshal."

"Custis," he said. "Call me Custis."

"All right. Then you have to call me Cindy," she said, her smile returning as she extended her hand. "Deal?"

"Deal."

Longarm walked over to his window and gazed

down on the street below with a lot of things now on his mind. The first order of business was to find out who the wild redheaded man was who had gone berserk down on Colfax Avenue. And once that man was either in jail . . . or dead . . . the second order of business was to find out who this sonofabitch called Bradley was. And that wouldn't be too difficult because Longarm really did have some good friends at the Mint who were high up the ladder of authority. And then when he found and met Bradley, Longarm was somehow and some way gonna get a little revenge of his own even if Cindy never found out about it.

"Custis?"

"I'm just thinking," he said over his shoulder.

And Longarm was thinking hard. A man like himself from West Virginia had been brought up to treat women properly. And if there was one thing that a man of his cloth could not abide, it was some egotistical gutter rat blackmailing a good and decent woman. Miss Cindy Allison had been honest enough to admit that she was no lady . . . but even a blind man could see that she was strong and courageous. A woman prepared to do whatever it took to save her parents' beloved Arizona ranch.

That was plenty good enough to make her a lady by Longarm's definition. And a blackmailer like Bradley was every bit as bad as a common scum-sucking wife-beating sonofabitch. A creature of the lowest form and barely a notch above a child molester in Longarm's considered opinion.

Yep, Cindy might have some distant get-even plan in the back of her mind, but Longarm's intentions toward Bradley were a whole lot more immediate.

Chapter 3

Longarm really did have a special date that Friday evening, but he completely forgot about it. To ease Cindy's pain, he had started pouring them both a little "liquid medicinal therapy." By that, he meant some good old brain-bustin' Kentucky whiskey. Then, one thing had led to another, and after quite a bit of the whiskey medicinal, he found himself standing over a very naked and lovely Arizona cowgirl whose sky blue eyes were glued to his big and quite stiff manhood.

"Cindy, are you sure that you are up to this?" he asked, concerned about maybe taking advantage of the same woman who was already being taken advantage of by a government skunk named Bradley.

"I'm obviously not as up to it as you are," Cindy said with a giggle as she reached out and took his throbbing rod in her hand.

"But, Cindy, you've lost blood and you're . . ."

"I'm a strong woman bred and raised on a ranch," she argued, hands working on his throbbing tool, "and

I'm not drunk or being blackmailed. What I am wanting is *you*, Custis. Are you wanting me bad, too?"

He sat on the bed and drew her close. "Is the sky blue?"

"Then let's stop all the conversation and get right down to business," she murmured, bending over and taking Longarm in her mouth.

He sighed with pleasure and wound his fingers into her long blond hair. "That's real nice."

"It's about to get even nicer," Cindy promised as she pushed him onto his back and then began to suck his rod with great enthusiasm and skill.

Longarm groaned and let himself enjoy the moment. He closed his eyes and let the waves of pleasure rise higher and higher, and when he could stand no more, he gently eased her off him, and then spread Cindy's silken thighs and returned the favor she had given.

Cindy was no longer in any pain from her bullet wound. Quite the opposite. She squealed and thrashed, but he pinned her to the mattress until she begged him to stop and mount her.

"With pleasure," he grunted, slipping his big rod into her wetness.

Cindy was a wildcat in bed. She thrashed and bucked and hollered so loudly that Longarm had to silence her with fierce kisses so as not to disturb all the occupants of his rooming house. And when they both finally reached the absolute pinnacle of their pleasure, Longarm and the young woman seemed to melt into each other until they were one heaving mass of flesh and fire.

At last, Longarm pumped the remainder of his seed

into the Arizona cowgirl, and then fell over panting and grinning. "Now *that*," he said, "was about as good as I've had in many a moon."

Cindy laughed. "I'll bet you say that to a different woman every night."

"Nope. Only every other night."

She jabbed him hard with her elbow, and paid the price as pain shot up through that bullet wound. "Ouch! That was sure stupid of me."

"Are you all right?" he asked, afraid that her wound might have reopened during their rousing romp.

She studied her bandage. "I don't think I reopened it. But I probably ought to be a little more careful."

Longarm sat up on his bed as naked as when he was born. He handed Cindy another drink and took a sip of his own. "If you're that good when you're convalescing, I can't wait to take you when you are completely healthy."

"Oh, I'm plenty healthy." Cindy tossed down her good Kentucky whiskey. "And to tell you the truth, I'd nearly forgotten how good a *real* man can make me feel."

"Meaning that Bradley isn't much of a man?"

"That's right. He's petty and peevish, for lack of a better word. And he's real fussy. He wants to screw me all the time, but he's so quick and prissy about it that I never felt satisfied . . . only used. Once, I told him he was so fast I ought to just use my hand, but he didn't like that and got angry. And another time, I started calling him 'Jackrabbit' and he sure didn't like that, but I kept it up and still do. It's a small revenge, but it's something."

"I'm going to make sure that you never have to lay down for him again," Longarm promised.

Her brow furrowed. "But I might get fired if you interfere."

"I'll figure out a way to make sure that doesn't happen," Longarm told her. "I'm going to put some time to the problem and come up with a solution that you'll like."

"I like you," she said. "Can I stay here with you all weekend?"

"You sure can."

"But I have to go to my apartment and feed my cat. He's going to be upset that I'm missing and out of both water and food."

"I could do that," Longarm offered. "Just tell me where you live and give me the key."

"I'd rather go with you," Cindy told him. "Pedro needs a lot of attention."

"His name is Pedro?"

"Yes. He's a yellow tomcat and his tail is bobbed. I don't know if someone did that on purpose or if he got his tail caught in a door or a rattrap. But anyway, he's been my only friend in this city."

"I'm gonna be your friend," Longarm told her.

"And lover."

"Yes," he readily agreed, running his big hand over her flat stomach and then down to the wet, hairy place that had just given him so much pleasure. "That, too, as long as you want."

"I want," Cindy whispered, pressing his hand against her wetness. "I want a lot."

Longarm beamed. "You know, you're quite a

woman. Most women would still be half in shock from being wounded, but not you. Cindy Allison, you've got grit."

"So do you, Marshal. You saved my life and maybe the lives of a lot of other people on Colfax Avenue this morning. Do you think that man who shot me got away clean?"

"I don't know. When we go out to eat a little later, I need to stop by the police station and find out if that red-haired maniac was shot or escaped without being arrested."

"What do you think set him off like that?"

"I have no idea," Longarm confessed. "Sometimes, people just mentally snap. And like I said, he might have been aiming for me and you were just unfortunate to have been in his line of fire. But either way, I'm going to make sure that he is either dead, or arrested and sent to prison for a good long while."

Cindy closed her eyes and sighed. "I'm suddenly so tired, Custis."

He got off the bed and covered her with a sheet and blanket. "Why don't you sleep and I'll go get some food and find out about that crazy man. Later, if you're feeling up to it, we can go to your apartment and feed that tomcat you seem to be so fond of."

"I'd like to sleep awhile. You and the whiskey are a very potent combination."

"Are you complaining already?"

"No," she said, smiling. "I'm not complaining a bit. In fact, you and the whiskey were exactly what I needed, and will need again before too much time passes."

"That's music to my ears," Longarm said. "Now go to sleep for a while. I'll lock the door on my way out and return within an hour with food and hopefully the news that the redheaded man was shot dead."

"Custis? The key to my apartment is in my coin purse. Maybe you ought to stop by and feed Pedro." She gave Longarm her address, and he knew that it was only a few blocks away. Then she added, "And please take a few minutes to pet the little fellow. You'll like him."

"I hope so. I've always been partial to dogs and horses."

She yawned and stretched, then purred, "Well, maybe you just haven't met the right pussycats."

Longarm caught her meaning and chuckled. "Maybe you're right, Cindy. Maybe you're right."

Longarm pulled on his coat and buckled on his gun belt. He was six feet four, and sported a handlebar mustache. Broad of shoulder, he was a study in ruggedness, and he wore a brown tweed coat and vest, blue gray shirt with a shoestring tie, and low-heeled boots of cordovan leather. The gun he was strapping on was a double-action Colt Model T, caliber .44-.40, and he wore it on his left hip, butt forward. As a backup, he had a twin-barreled derringer of the same caliber that was cleverly attached to his watch fob. This derringer had saved his life more than once when, covered by a gun, he had asked to see the exact time of his death and had whipped out and fired the weapon.

Now, with Cindy's address imprinted on his mind and her key in his vest pocket, he headed out onto the street. He decided that he would visit Pedro first, and then head over to the local police station on his way back to his rooming house in order to find out about the redheaded maniac.

It took Longarm less than ten minutes to arrive at Cindy Allison's rooming house, and he noted that she, like himself, lived on the second floor. The neighborhood where she lived could be kindly described as humble. In actuality, it was nearly a slum, and in a very poor part of Denver where prostitution and street crimes were commonplace. But the rents were dirt cheap, and there was a street lamp right outside the house's door.

"She lives damn frugally," he said to himself. "This isn't a good place for a young woman to stay all on her own."

Longarm had a scowl on his face as he entered the building and began to ascend the stairway. Two intoxicated and ragged fellows were lying on the steps, and seemed to have no interest in moving so that he could pass.

"Move aside," Longarm growled. "Or I'll kick both your drunken asses down the stairs!"

The two men tried to focus on the towering United States marshal, and when they did, they realized that he was not bluffing and was entirely capable of carrying out his threat.

"Ain't no way to talk to a fella that rough," one of them managed to whine. "Ain't good manners to speak that way to a couple of men that life has dealt such a cruel hand."

Longarm glared down at them. "What's the matter with you two? Neither one of you can be over thirty. You boys ought to be out earning a living instead of dead drunk in some lousy apartment house stairway.

Take a solid hold on your lives and make something out of your worthless selves!"

"Who the hell are you to be tellin' us what to do!" came the whiny response. "We've been dealt all of life's most awful unfairness. More than you can imagine even!"

Longarm brought out his wallet and displayed his badge. "You want to give me trouble and wind up in jail? How would that be for yet more of life's unfairness?"

They both clamped their mouths shut, and one of them finished off a bottle of cheap wine with a few rapid swallows.

"All right then," Longarm said, hardly able to bear their stench. "Get out of here and don't let me see either you on my way back down."

"You moved in here?" one stammered, eyes flitting from Longarm back to his partner. "We didn't see you move in here."

"I figure there's a whole lot you can't see," Longarm told them with disgust. "Now both of you just git!"

The two half crawled and half stumbled down the stairway and out the door below. One of them shouted something crude and uncomplimentary at Longarm from the street, but he ignored the insult and came to stand outside Cindy Allison's quarters. He inserted the key into the lock and opened the door to see a rather large, heavyset man lounging on a couch wearing only a fancy bathrobe, mostly open to the crotch, and matching slippers.

"What the—" the man cried, jumping to his feet. "Mister, who the hell are you!"

It was, Longarm knew without a doubt, Bradley. The government official was no doubt waiting for Cindy, and had already undressed anticipating a late afternoon session of coercive sex.

Longarm closed the door behind him and folded his muscular arms across his chest. He decided that the less Bradley actually knew about him, the better.

"I said who are you and what are you doing here!" Bradley shouted, standing, fists doubling at his sides.

Longarm just smiled. "Do you live here?"

"No, I do not! But you don't either and you'd better get out of here fast, or I'll throw you out and then call the police!"

"Is that what you're going to do next, Jackrabbit?" Longarm asked in a soft voice that was utterly chilling. He took a few steps closer to the blackmailing bureaucrat and grinned. "Nice robe and slippers. Real pretty, I'd say."

The robe was either silk or satin. It was loosely tied with a little cord and burgundy-colored, with matching soft slippers. Longarm sized the man up in an instant. Bradley was a six-footer, but soft, with a receding hairline. He looked to be pushing forty; however, there was enough of a hump in his broad shoulders to tell Longarm that Bradley was not a complete weakling.

"You'd better go," Bradley said, advancing a step and raising a fist. "I'm warning you, mister!"

Longarm took two quick steps forward and, to Bradley's surprise and consternation, he grabbed the cord and opened the man's robe to reveal a potbelly and a little rosebud hiding in a sparse crop of pubic hair.

"What the hell you doing!" Bradley cried, eyes

flooding with sudden fear as he retied the robe and re-treated so fast, he stepped out of one of his pretty slippers. "Mister, I don't—"

Longarm chuckled. Bradley had been humiliated just as he'd intended. "You sure got a short little dinger there, Bradley. But then, Cindy told me that it was only about three inches long and thin as a damned pencil."

Something moved out of the corner of Longarm's eye, and he saw it was the yellow bobtailed cat named Pedro. The cat seemed very interested in what was about to happen next. He jumped up on a table, licked his lips, and watched Longarm with curious green eyes.

Bradley swallowed hard. "Mister, I don't know who you are or what you want . . . but if it's money . . . you can have all that's in my wallet there on the table. Just . . . just go away!"

"Why, Jackrabbit," Longarm said almost jokingly. "I thought we might have ourselves a little private fun!" Longarm hooked his thumbs in his gun belt.

Bradley paled. "I'm getting my clothes and I'm leaving!" He grabbed a letter opener and held it out in front of him to defend himself. The letter opener looked sharp, and Longarm knew that it would have been a real weapon in the hands of a street fighter. But in Bradley's soft hand, it was no threat at all.

Longarm jumped forward. He batted the letter opener aside with his left hand, and with his right open hand, he slapped the government worker so hard that Bradley stumbled back across the room with a split and bleeding lip.

Gone was the bluster and all pretense of making a fight. "Oh, please, mister! Don't kill or hurt me!"

Longarm could see that Bradley was sufficiently terrified. He picked up the letter opener and waved it in Bradley's face. "Get out of here right now before I lose control and do something real bad to you! If we ever meet again here, I'll castrate you like a fat market hog!"

Bradley nodded, his double chins quivering. "Just let me get my clothes and wallet, then—"

"Get out now while you can!" Longarm roared, advancing another step and grinning like a crazy killer.

Now completely out of his mind with fear, Bradley pissed all over his leg and the nice burgundy robe. His yellow stream ran down both legs and soaked into his pretty soft slippers, too.

"Go!" Longarm said, advancing on the trembling man.

Bradley shot past him and out the door. Longarm closed it and burst into laughter. Pedro, the tomcat, moved gracefully over to his bowl and meowed that he was hungry and would like some more cat food. When Longarm found the food and filled his bowl, the cat arched his back and purred.

Some tough tomcat, Longarm thought with amusement. He's about as tough as poor old Bradley.

Longarm went to the dirty window and looked down on the street. He saw Bradley clumsily trying to hold his robe tight to his body while running up the sidewalk. Every few feet, Bradley would glance back as if an avenging angel was chasing him.

That made Longarm laugh out loud. He put his hands on his hips and surveyed Cindy Allison's room. It was very, very spartan. Just a bed, table, two chairs, and an old used-up couch. But the place was spotless and very clean. The floor was hand-scrubbed and polished to a shine.

On the scarred table was a daguerreotype, and it showed a family of four. In the picture, Cindy looked to be about fourteen years old, and her father well past forty. He was a tall, thin man with a battered hat and a face deeply lined by sun and wind. Cindy's mother was also tall and thin, with a brave smile and a simple dress that probably had been made from bleached and dyed feed sacks.

Longarm studied the boy he recalled being named Monty. Monty stood just apart from his family. He was a miniature of his father, but his face wasn't lined and it wasn't innocent like that of the other three in the picture. Rather, there was a belligerence and toughness that belied his youth. Longarm had seen boys this young wear this look on their faces before, and it almost always spelled future trouble.

Bad trouble.

Monty, Longarm could see at a glance, was a hard case even at six years of age. A boy with defiance already stamped on his face. Defiance coupled with anger. No wonder, Longarm thought, that the kid had already gone bad.

Pedro meowed and jumped up on the table. Longarm figured the little guy wanted to be petted, and he was right. Soon, Pedro was purring up a storm.

"I don't think that your lady is going to live here much longer," Longarm told the tomcat. "It's too rough and too dangerous. I'm gonna have to help her find a better and safer place. Maybe even my own rooms for a while. Will that suit you, Pedro?"

In response, the tomcat moved over to the edge of the table and brushed up against Longarm.

"I guess it will then," Longarm said. "I'll be back for you. Don't eat all that food up at once."

Longarm took one quick look around, and saw a few clothes on a rack and a cheap cardboard suitcase. He decided to grab Cindy a change of clothes and her few personal belongings. He crammed them all in the suitcase, and even thought about adding the cat, but decided against it.

"Later, Pedro," he called as he headed out the door intent on stopping at the police station and finding out about the crazy redhead.

Chapter 4

The local chief of detectives was Pete Barstow, and Longarm had often worked with the man and his department. Barstow was in his early fifties, not physically imposing, but he was fearless, smart and incorruptible. He had a well trained and dedicated staff of detectives who kept the criminals from taking over that part of the city. He was tough, but fair, and he was not a man to be trifled with. Longarm knew that Barstow had personally shot and killed more a half dozen men in open gunfights. He walked with a limp from a bullet he'd taken in the knee during the early years of his career.

When Longarm entered the station, and was escorted to Barstow's cluttered little office, he knew that he would be greeted warmly and dealt with honestly. And that, Longarm knew, was a luxury because very often federal and local authorities were in competition, and cooperation was rare because politics rather often trumped professionalism.

"So, Custis Long, what brings you here today?" Barstow pointed to the cheap and battered suitcase in Longarm's hand. "Did you get kicked out of another woman's place and need a place to lay over here while the passions die?"

"Hell, no!"

"You come to work for me? I'll make sure that you're appreciated in my station and you'll start at the top of our pay scale."

"Thank you kindly for the offer, but I like my job," Longarm told the man. "And as for this suitcase, it belongs to the woman who was shot and wounded over on Colfax Avenue this morning."

Barstow climbed out of his office chair and shook Longarm's hand. "Yes, I heard about that and you were recognized. Where did you take that attractive young woman? I'd like to have her interviewed. Maybe she can help us catch the gunman."

"I can tell you all that you need to know about him," Longarm said. "After all, I'm the one who returned his fire and I'm dead sure that I put a bullet in his shoulder."

"He couldn't have been wounded too badly," Barstow mused. "Because he kept running down Colfax randomly firing his gun at the morning crowd. He created a real panic. Some people got trampled, and he shot and killed someone who got in his way. We want him real bad, Custis."

"I heard his gunshots," Longarm said. "Did he get away clean?"

"I'm afraid so," Barstow replied. "I've got my best men trying to track that man down. So far, no luck. It's as if he just evaporated like smoke."

"Did you check out all the hospitals and doctors' offices?" Longarm asked. "He'd need some serious medical attention due to that bullet I put in his shoulder."

"We did," Barstow answered. "But the man never sought medical attention. Maybe your bullet hit him high in the shoulder and passed right through."

"That's possible," Longarm said. "Everything happened real fast."

"Custis, I was hoping you'd show up today, because we need your statement on the shootings and want the best description you can give us about him."

"He was a real big man with a red beard and matching hair. The beard was full and his hair was long and wild, like that of an Apache Indian except for the color."

"Was the shooter taller than you?"

"I'd say so, by an inch maybe," Longarm decided. "But he was certainly heavier than me. He had a barrel chest and legs like tree trunks. I'll bet the man weighed close to three hundred pounds, but he was fast and agile."

"What about his age?"

Longarm thought about that for a moment. "I'd guess he was in his mid-thirties, Pete."

"Is there anything that you can remember about him that would give us some clue as to his person or whereabouts?"

Longarm knew what Pete Barstow was fishing for by this question. The town marshal was hoping for some distinguishing feature that would give him a hint as to the red-haired man's occupation or origin.

"I'm afraid that I can't help you," Longarm said.

"The main things I noticed about him, other than his great size, were his wild red hair and eyes that looked real crazy."

"Blue eyes?"

"Yes," Longarm said, "pale blue."

"And you'd never seen him on the streets before?"

"No," Longarm replied. "And if I had, I would have remembered someone that stood out so much from the crowd."

Barstow frowned. "So far, nobody that was there this morning on Colfax during the shooting has been able to remember seeing this giant before. Either he came from another part of the city, or he might be a new arrival. Someone who just blew into town."

"And went on a killing spree," Longarm said. "Maybe he got some bad opium or drugs. I've seen people who smoked peyote go crazy with rage."

"Sure," Barstow said, "and how many times have we seen men go berserk after drinking too much bad liquor?"

"Too often," Longarm answered. "But this man definitely wasn't drunk. He was running and firing in a way that told me he had a clear mind and full coordination. No, he wasn't drunk."

"Do you think it was all just random? That you and the others down there on Colfax this morning were simply unfortunates in that you were in the wrong place at the wrong time?"

The question was a good one, and it caused Longarm to blink. "I'd like to think that. But . . ." Longarm's voice trailed off into silence.

"But what?" Barstow demanded. "Are you thinking that the red-haired shooter was after you or someone else in particular?"

Longarm glanced away, his mind suddenly latching on to a possible explanation that made sense of everything.

"Talk to me, Custis!"

Longarm turned back to his friend and said, "This morning after the shooting, I was thinking that perhaps the giant was after me. You know. All of us lawmen have sworn enemies. But what if someone wanted it all to look like the random killing of a United States marshal or a lowly government worker from Arizona?"

"Get to the point, Custis."

"I'm wondering if I was the real target this morning."

"If you weren't, then who was?" Barstow asked impatiently.

"Miss Cindy Allison, the girl that was wounded in the upper arm and who I took to a doctor's office right after the shooting."

"I need to interview her," Pete said. "Where is she now?"

"At my rooms," Longarm said, eyes dropping to the floor.

"Your rooms, huh?"

"Yeah."

He pointed. "And that's her suitcase?"

"Yep."

Pete Barstow shook his head. "Custis, I know your reputation with the ladies, but this must set the all-time record for seduction. For crying out loud! Miss Allison gets shot this morning, and you've probably already screwed her!"

Longarm made a sour face, but kept silent.

"I'm right on all counts, aren't I," Barstow said with a mixture of wonder and contempt. "My gosh, Custis, you are a real piece of work."

"It isn't exactly like you're thinking."

Barstow's eyebrows shot up in question. "Oh? And why is that?"

"Well, I just wanted to help her out. She's a poor ranch girl from Arizona and the place she's been living is a crime-ridden slum."

"So you save her life and now you're giving her a home and your bed?"

"Only for a while," Longarm said a mite sheepishly.

"Until you get tired of screwing her and need your rooms for a new conquest."

Longarm scowled. "I don't like the way you put things, Pete. If I hadn't of stepped into that shooting gallery this morning, she probably would have been shot dead. And after that, I pulled her out of the street a moment before she'd have been run over by a freight wagon."

"Well, maybe the freight wagon driver was also trying to kill her . . . or make sure that she was dead. That is, if she was indeed the real target of the shootings."

"You may have just hit on something," Longarm admitted.

"Do you remember anything about the freight wagon so that we can check it out as a possibility?" the detective asked.

"As a matter of fact, I do," Longarm answered. "The wagon was carrying sacks of grain and bales of grass hay. It had a name on the side and as it passed, I seem to recall it was from a livery stable here in town."

"There are a lot of livery stables in Denver," Barstow told him. "Can't you remember which one it was?"

"No. But the name was written in big red letters on the side of the wagon's bed. And for some reason I recall that the front right wheel . . . the one that nearly ran over Cindy . . . was missing a spoke."

Barstow popped up from behind his desk and reached for his hat and gun belt. "With that much information, I'm certain we can find that wagon if it's still here in Denver."

"You're going to do the search personally?"

"I am," Barstow told him. "All my men are either looking for the red-haired killer or else off duty. And the wagon could be on its way out of town, so I want to get on this immediately."

Longarm set Cindy's suitcase down beside the lawman's desk. "Mind if I tag along?"

"I was expecting that," Barstow muttered, moving around his desk and passing Longarm on his way out of the office. "Do you recall anything about the driver of that freight wagon?"

"Only that he had a black beard, a foul mouth, and a bullwhip in his left fist."

"A bullwhip-cracking lefty! Ha! This is getting better by the minute! Come along, Custis! We're going to find that driver and . . . if it really was a conspiracy to murder that Arizona girl . . . then the driver will lead us directly to that red-haired sonofabitch."

Despite his shattered knee, Pete Barstow could walk damned fast, and Longarm had to stretch his much longer legs just to keep pace with the local lawman. As soon as they were out on the street and hurrying along toward the closest livery, Pete asked, "Any idea why they might want to kill the young lady that you just saved and then conveniently bedded?"

Longarm ignored the gibe. "I'm not aware of any motive. But . . ."

Pete stopped abruptly on the sidewalk. "But what, Custis?"

"Miss Allison is in Denver trying to raise money to save her family's cattle ranch in Arizona."

"And if she failed to raise money, what would happen?"

"Her family would lose it in bankruptcy, I suppose."

Pete threw up his hands. "So, if Miss Allison is the *only* hope they have of getting cash . . . and if she were accidentally shot or run over . . . then someone would probably get her family's ranch for a song?"

"I guess they would, Pete."

"So we have a motive! A damn strong motive as a matter of fact."

"Maybe," Longarm agreed. "But right now, it's all speculation. Just a theory."

"My theories usually turn out to be correct," Pete said, briskly moving off down the sidewalk again. "So let's see if that holds true this time. Let's find the driver and then the red-haired bastard and I'll make him talk before I—"

"No threats," Longarm cautioned. "We're sworn to uphold the law . . . not to be judge and jury and executioner."

"Sure thing," Pete replied, figuring that he was going to do what was right and the law be damned.

Chapter 5

"How many stables do you reckon there are in Denver?"
Longarm asked the detective.

"Oh, about a dozen."

"Then maybe we should split up and each take half
of 'em," Longarm suggested.

Barstow stopped and frowned as he considered the
suggestion. After a moment, he shook his head. "Naw."

"Why not?" Longarm demanded, knowing that Barstow was the local authority and would have the final
call on this decision. "I mean, you said that there's a
chance that freight wagon is headed out of Denver. If
that's the case, we need to move as fast as we can."

"I know what I said, Custis. But it's far more likely
that the wagon is still in Denver. And the other thing is
that, if the driver and the wounded shooter are together,
I'd like to have you as a backup."

"All right," Longarm conceded. "But we could do
this twice as fast if we split up."

"Yeah, and if you were the one that found the big

man, you'd most likely finish what you started with a bullet."

"Would that be so wrong?"

"No, but it seems to me that this pair we're hunting might not be the only ones that are involved . . . especially if they really want to kill your new Arizona roommate. You know, the damsel you saved in distress."

"Cut it out," Longarm snapped. "Let's get busy and see if we can cover all the stables before sundown."

"I'll keep up with you," Barstow promised.

Longarm hoped they would find the wagon a lot sooner than later. Pete Barstow would never admit the fact, but his knee was killing him right now and covering every livery in town was going to be a sheer torment for the limping lawman.

They visited five livery stables before they approached the one on Market Street. It was a run-down business that looked to be doing poorly. There were a half dozen underfed horses in the corrals, and the hay that was stacked nearby would not have been appealing even to a starving Texas longhorn. The barn was falling down, as were the corral fences, and there were two mangy dogs tied to a stake driven in the ground beside the front barn doors. Both dogs were large and mean looking, and they watched the two strangers with fierce and suspicious intensity.

"Custis, do any of those old freight wagons look like the one that we're after?" Barstow asked, motioning toward a line of derelict wagons.

Longarm angled toward the wagons, none of which

looked fit to roll. But when he came to the last one, mostly hidden behind the others, his face split with a wide grin. "This is the one, Pete."

The Denver detective nodded, and his hand moved toward the gun resting on his hip. Longarm had never seen the man pull iron, but he'd heard that Barstow shot straight and fast.

"Let's see who's inside the barn," Barstow suggested.

As they neared the barn, the two guard dogs jumped up and began to bark and growl with the hair on their necks standing up.

"They look serious," Longarm said.

"Indeed they do," Barstow agreed as the two dogs set up a frantic ruckus. "But those mongrels are no more serious than we are."

"I don't think we can squeeze our way through that front door without killing those dogs."

Pete halted and weighed the situation a moment before saying, "Let's go around to the back of the building. I never knew a livery barn that didn't have a rear set of drive through doors."

"And if this place doesn't have 'em," Longarm said, "we can just kick out a few boards and walk through the wall. The whole place is leaning and about to fall down."

"You got that right," Pete said as they changed direction.

The two guard dogs were really going crazy and snapping at their tethers.

"Whoever owns those dogs isn't a friendly man," Longarm observed. "Dogs that mean have got to have been mistreated from the time they were pups."

"I agree."

Longarm and Barstow started around the barn with every intention of leaving the two guard dogs to bark and raise a harmless ruckus. But halfway around the barn, Longarm heard a scrambling noise and turned to see that the dogs had been set free and were heading toward him and Barstow.

"Damn!" Longarm swore, his hand flashing to the gun on his hip.

Longarm's first bullet killed the lead dog with a shot to the head. Barstow's gun barked an instant later, and it kicked up dirt in front of the second dog, which had a remarkable change of attitude. Skidding on all fours, the dog swapped ends in mid-stride and lit out as if its tail was on fire.

"The second one was the smartest of the pair," Barstow dryly observed.

"You missed him," Longarm said with surprise. "And I'd always heard that you were a crack shot."

"I am," Barstow replied. "I missed that second one on purpose because I didn't think his heart was really in the fight."

"Sure you did," Longarm said, not believing a word of it.

"I did! The second one just didn't look as mean and determined as the first, so I gave him a chance to change his mean attitude and he did."

"Yeah, right."

Barstow said, "Now that those dogs are gone, we might as well go in the front door."

"If the driver with the bullwhip that seemed intent on

running Cindy over is inside, he might be hiding inside ready to kill us."

"You worried, Custis?"

"Nope. But I'm not walking through those front barn doors when there's a good possibility that someone is waiting for us in the dark with a big double-barreled shotgun."

"You make a good point," Barstow conceded. "So, what do you suggest?"

Longarm studied at the wall. "These boards are barely hanging on to their warped studs. I say we kick 'em in and dive through the wall with our guns at the ready."

"I like that idea. Let's do it!"

Both men reared back and kicked the boards, which offered no more resistance than expected. With a sudden hole in the barn, the two lawmen dove through the new opening with their guns up and ready to fire.

The deafening blast of a shotgun was followed by twin flashes that lit up the dark interior of the big stable. Longarm felt the sting of shot slash across his forearm, and he instinctively fired at where he'd seen the shotgun muzzle flash. Pete Barstow did exactly the same.

They heard a yelp and then a curse, followed by the sound of hard running feet.

"He's getting away!" Barstow shouted. "Go after him!"

Longarm was already up and moving. He was younger and faster than Pete, and he knew it was up to him to overtake and either arrest or kill whoever had just unloaded on them from inside the dilapidated livery barn.

He burst out the front door, and saw the thin freight wagon driver with the black beard rounding a corner and disappearing up the street toward the South Platte River. The man was a swift runner, and Longarm was damned unhappy about the prospect of having to chase after him for a long distance.

But there wasn't any choice in the matter. Running hard and fast, he rounded the corner, almost tripping over the cowering livery guard dog they had scared off with bullets. Longarm caught a glimpse of the man he was after disappearing into an alley about a block ahead.

Longarm cursed in anger.

When he reached the alley, he immediately realized it was a dead end bordered by dirty brick buildings. There was no way out and the tall buildings made the alley dim. There was a hellish mix of mosquitoes, swarming houseflies, and big biting horseflies gorging on garbage heaped in rotting mounds. It was a bad place to make a fight and an even worse place to die.

Longarm had a feeling that either he or the cornered freighter was going to die here, and he vowed that he would emerge the survivor.

"I know you're in here, mister. There's no way out and I'm not going away, so you might as well come out with your hands in the air. I just want you to answer a few questions. There is no reason for either of us to start swapping lead."

His suggestion was greeted with silence.

Longarm swatted at the damned swarming insects buzzing around his face. He had a strong aversion to both flies and mosquitoes. He'd been bitten by both far too often, and he'd be damned if he could figure out why God had put the miserable and filthy little bastards on this planet.

"You hear me, mister! If you don't come out, then I'm coming in after you."

"Who the hell are you!" a voice cried from somewhere in the darkest part of the alley.

"I'm Deputy United States Marshal Custis Long."

"I didn't do nothin' wrong! What you want with me?"

"I want to talk to you. Just talk. Now come on out."

"I . . . I don't think so, Marshal. I believe you intend to kill me, so I ain't comin' out and you should just go away and leave me alone."

Longarm cursed to himself, his mind churning furiously. "Dammit, man, I need to know why you tried to run over that woman on Colfax Avenue this morning."

There was a long pause of silence followed by, "I don't know what the hell you're talkin' about!"

"Sure you do! I saw you and I saw your damned freight wagon this morning. You were trying to run that young woman down and I want to know why." Longarm yelled. "Now, you got the choice to come outa hiding dead or alive. Which is it going to be?"

"Come and git me, you badge-totin' sonofabitch!"

"All right then," Longarm muttered to himself as he swatted again and again at the swarming insects that were starting to eat him alive. "I'm in no mood to wait around for you to get smart."

Longarm burst into a running crouch. A shot whip-cracked through the thick, fetid air, and the flies and mosquitoes were so damned thick that Longarm figured a few had to have taken his bullet. He saw a rusting old piece of junk, and dove in behind it just as more bullets split the stinking air.

Longarm took a few deep breaths, sucking up a bug through one of his nostrils. He choked and pushed a thumb over one nostril and blew hard with the other, expelling the little invader. Then he raised his head and tried to find his target. Not finding it but wanting to test his adversary's mettle, Longarm fired twice in the man's general direction.

His shots must have been close to the mark, because the man he was after yelled, "All right! I surrender!"

"You're a hell of a lot smarter than you look," Longarm called out to the man. "Throw down your weapon and come out with your hands reaching for the sky."

The freight wagon driver appeared as a dim outline with his hands upraised.

"Come forward slow and easy."

"These mosquitoes are killin' me!"

"Well, mister," Longarm answered, "they ain't doing me any favors either. So the sooner you come out, the sooner we both get out of this gawdamn alley."

The man lowered his hand to slap an insect on his face, and that almost cost him his life. Longarm grabbed the thin man and shoved him back toward the opening of the alley. "Move!"

Once they were out of that stinking, insect-filled alley, Longarm took a good look at the man he'd just chased down. There was no doubt he had the right wagon freighter.

"Why'd you try to kill that young lady?" Longarm hissed.

"I didn't!" the man wailed.

"Well, you sure as hell didn't try to draw up that team or reach for the wagon's brake."

The freighter shifted uneasily. "Marshal, the truth is that I was still half drunk from last night and I didn't have my wits about me. When that woman fell, I was looking off in another direction and just couldn't react in time to slow the wagon."

"I don't believe you," Longarm told the man. "You can tell your lies to Detective Barstow after we lock you up in jail."

"On what charge?"

"Attempted murder sounds real good to me," Longarm told the man with grim satisfaction. "And I think Barstow will go along with that charge without a second thought."

"You can't do that!"

"Watch us," Longarm hissed, giving the man a hard shove backward. "Now, move before I lose my patience with you and put a bullet in your lying mouth."

Barstow was waiting by the barn. As Longarm and his prisoner approached, he hurried forward saying, "There was no one else inside. This was the only one in the barn."

"I thought you were thieves trying to rob or kill me," the man wheezed, eyes shifting down toward his feet. "That's why I opened up on you with the shotgun. I was just tryin' to defend my poor and innocent self. I was just trying to stay alive."

"Where is the big man with the red hair and beard?" Barstow demanded.

The driver pretended to look around. "What . . . what are you talkin' about?"

Barstow was a direct man with a direct style of inter-
rogating criminals. His hand latched around the thin
man's neck, and he began to squeeze until the freighter's
eyes bulged and the thin man started choking.

"Answer me straight, you skinny asshole! Do it or
I'll throttle you like I would a barnyard chicken for the
pot!"

Barstow slammed his victim up against a building
and bore down even harder on the freighter's throat.

Longarm laid a hand on his friend's rigid forearm.
"Pete, if you don't ease up a mite on his gullet, you're
going to break his neck and we'll never learn anything
from him about the redheaded shooter."

Barstow released the pressure and the freighter
sagged to the ground, choking and whooping for air.
They gave him a full minute to recover, and then both
Barstow and Longarm knelt down and studied their victim intently.

"You better talk," Longarm advised. "Because if
Detective Barstow doesn't break your neck . . . I damn
sure will."

"Please . . . please just leave me alone! I didn't do
anything wrong," the man said in a strangled voice. "I'm
just a poor, innocent workingman."

"You're poor all right," Longarm said. "You're a
damned poor liar is what you are." He drew his gun and
cocked back the hammer "Now, tell us where the red
haired man is that did the shooting this morning, or prepare to meet Satan."

"Don't shoot me! I'll tell you whatever you want to
know!" the man screeched.

"One more lie out of that ugly mouth and it's time for you to visit Satan," Barstow gravely pronounced.

"The man that you want has a bullet wound in his shoulder," the freighter stammered.

"And I'm the one that put it there this morning," Longarm said. "Now tell me where we can find him or prepare to die!"

"I don't know! Please, I'm telling you both the truth!"

Longarm was having none of it. "I'll give you until the count of three to tell us where he is, and then I'm gonna blow what few brains you have all over this wall. One. Two."

"He's . . . he's leaving town! The red-haired giant called himself Cain. He got a doctor to dig out his bullet and bandage his wound. Then he rode out of town this afternoon on a half-broke sorrel gelding that I sold him not more than two or three hours ago."

"Where is Cain headed?" Barstow demanded.

"I think maybe he's riding for Arizona."

"You *think* he's riding to Arizona, or you *know* he's riding to Arizona?" Longarm pressed.

"All I'm sure of is that he was from Arizona and he told me that he was going back there when he had finished up his business here in Denver."

"What part of the Arizona Territory did he hail from?" Barstow asked. "That's a big chunk of country."

"Cain said he was from down near Yuma and he liked to go down to Mexico for tequila and them hot little border señoritas. The only reason I even know that much is because we got drunk one night and Cain started telling me stories about the Yuma Prison. Cain bragged about how he murdered another inmate there and they never found him out. He was real proud of beating a fellow prisoner to death with his fists. He said it was a famous Mexican bandito named Manuel Escobar who claimed to have killed more than ten men with his knife."

Longarm glanced over at Barstow. "What do you think? Is he telling us the truth?"

"Maybe, but I don't think this bird ain't done singing yet," Barstow decided. "Let's take him to my jail and wring out the rest of what he knows about this Cain fella."

The freighter threw up his hands in supplication. "That's all I know about Cain! Honest!"

But Barstow wasn't buying any of that. He jerked his prisoner to his feet and then produced a pair of handcuffs. "Put your hands behind your back."

"I ain't done nothin' wrong!"

"According to Longarm, you tried to run over and kill a woman this morning. So get your hands behind your back or I'll break both of your damn shoulders!" Barstow growled.

When the man was properly handcuffed, Barstow shoved him to start him walking, and went limping after him. Longarm nodded with approval, then called out, "Pete?"

The man stopped and turned. "What?"

"I just wanted you to know that I appreciate your direct style of interrogation. Where'd you learn it?"

"You mean the neck squeeze?"

"Yeah, among other things."

"I learned it when I was a young law officer working up in the Colorado silver mines."

"Well," Longarm said with a grin, "I'm here to say that it's very much like my own technique. Works most every time."

"Yeah," Barstow agreed, "except when you get a little carried away and break a man's neck."

"Yeah," Longarm replied, following after them. "There is always that risk. So what about this Cain heading for Arizona?"

"My wages are paid by the citizens of Denver," Barstow said. "So if you want to bring Cain to justice, I'm afraid that you'll have to do it on your own."

"But he gunned down a citizen of Denver on Colfax Avenue this morning," Longarm countered. "Isn't that reason enough for you to put out a wanted poster on the man and a bounty for his arrest?"

"It is for a fact," Detective Barstow said. "And once I've gotten everything I can out of this weasel, I'll do just that. But I still can't go chasin' after Cain. I've got a lot of problems right here in town."

"Well, I can't either," Longarm said with disgust. "Cain is a killer and he needs to be brought to justice, but he didn't commit any federal offense, so my hands are tied in the matter."

"I can send a telegraph down to the Yuma Prison and see if we get anything back about Cain. His last name or real name would be helpful, and also it would be good to tell them that he was responsible for beating to death another prisoner named Manuel Escobar."

"Maybe they'll put a warrant out on him for Escobar's death, and someone down in Arizona will bring Cain to justice."

"Don't count on that," Barstow said. "Odds are that Cain will just go right on killing people until he gets either old or unlucky."

"Yeah," Longarm said, "but it sure galls me to think that he'll go on living and killing folks. And even worse, I'm really wondering if he was trying to kill Miss Allison."

"Yeah," Barstow said with a frown. "Maybe we'll find out the answer to that after I interrogate this prisoner awhile."

"I'll be by your jail later to help you out if need be," Longarm said.

"Oh," Barstow drawled, "I think I can handle it all by myself."

"Yeah, I'm sure that you can. Just don't kill him before I get another turn at asking him some questions."

"Fair enough," Barstow said. "Where you going to now?"

"I've got to retrieve Miss Allison's bag and then go back and see how she's doing."

Barstow winked. "I figured that was what you were up to next. Have a good time playing nursemaid, Custis."

Longarm scowled. "Peter, you got a filthy mind."

"Maybe," Barstow admitted, "but everyone in Denver knows that you've got quite the reputation with the ladies. I'm just wondering how long this Miss Allison is going to last before you get tired of her and set your sights on some other woman."

Longarm started to reply, then decided the man's comment didn't justify a response. Longarm *was* a bit fickle, and many women just bored him to death after he'd had his way with them for a night or two. But Cindy, Miss Allison, seemed to have a lot of character and intelligence, and he was concerned about the fact that the red giant might have been hired to kill her and make it look like something that had been done in a random, senseless manner. If that was the case, then Cindy's life could still be in great danger.

Longarm knew that he had to find out what was at the bottom of things, or it would slowly drive him crazy.

Chapter 6

Longarm and Cindy Allison reclaimed the yellow bob-tailed cat Pedro, and took up residence together at Longarm's rooms on Saturday. On Sunday afternoon, after yet another vigorous bout of lovemaking, they grew restless and decided to go for a walk.

"It's a fine, sunny afternoon and we should go out and get some fresh air," Longarm announced. "I think a good, vigorous stroll along Cherry Creek is in order."

Cindy blushed. "We've made love so often and so strenuously that I'm not sure that I can walk without appearing to be bowlegged. And don't you think that would be embarrassing to us both?"

"Not to me," Longarm proudly asserted. "Wear a dress and no one will be able to tell that you're walking a little bowlegged."

"Fair enough. Shall we have dinner on the town?"

"I'd like that," Longarm said. "My treat, of course."

"Of course. And you're not afraid of gossip about us or running into one of your many previous conquests?"

"I've never treated women badly," Longarm told her in complete truthfulness. "I've loved them and left them, but always with a smile and my best wishes. I'd like to think that I've never been thought of unkindly by my former lovers."

"Perhaps not," Cindy offered, "because it is very true that you are indeed a rare gentleman both in and out of bed. But I can't help but think that you've broken a lot of tender hearts."

He looked at her and said in his most gentle voice, "Cindy, please don't fall in love with me. I'm really not the marrying kind. I suspect there are plenty of men that say that and don't mean it . . . but I do."

"I know. You've told me that several times and I believe you. And I also know that you love your job and that I love ranching in Arizona. So while I'm aware that our paths must soon part, I'm still going to remember you always."

"As I will remember you," he said, kissing her lips. "Now, enough of this crass sentimentality. Let's get dressed and go for that stroll. Also, I want to stop by Detective Barstow's office and see if he received a response to his telegraph about that red-haired man named Cain."

"You mean a hoped-for response from the Yuma Prison?"

"Exactly."

"If the man is gone, then I don't see what can be done from right here in Denver."

"Plenty can be done," Longarm assured her. "Detective Pete Barstow has issued a warrant for the man's arrest on the charge of murder. And I'm sure there is some kind of reward on his head."

Cindy nodded with understanding and glanced at the bandage on her upper arm. "Without your heroics, and with a few more inches closer to my body, it would have been a *double* murder yesterday morning on Colfax."

"Let's hurry along to see if any news has been telegraphed from Yuma," Longarm said, grabbing his hat.

He did not want to tell this young woman that there was a chance that she had been specifically targeted by Cain in order to insure that her parents did not receive any more funds and thus would be unable to keep their small but valuable cattle ranch located along the Gila River. If Cindy really had been targeted by Cain, it meant that her parents and her brother might well be similarly targeted by the giant red-haired killer.

A short time later, they stood in the office of the chief of detectives. "As a matter of fact," a young detective mused thoughtfully as he rearranged a mess of papers strewn across Barstow's cluttered desk, "this office did receive a telegram from Yuma. Let me see where it is."

Longarm and Cindy patiently waited while the lawman searched through piles of correspondence and wanted posters.

"Oh, here it is. Detective Barstow wrote a note on the telegram. It says that you are to be contacted regarding this telegram at your office first thing tomorrow morning."

Longarm took the telegram from the deputy and read it aloud to Cindy. "This message was sent in response on Saturday afternoon by the head warden at the Yuma Prison. This is what it says:

> *Denver Detective Barstow. Regarding former convict Cain Hawker. Appreciate knowing he beat to death our inmate Manuel Escobar. Not surprised and good riddance. Based on description provided, convict Cain Hawker is your shooter. Red-haired giant imprisoned here for multiple murders, rape, extortion, assaults, train and stagecoach robbery. Was sentenced to hang, but escaped two months ago. Strangled my two toughest and most experienced prison guards. Swam Colorado River to freedom on California side. Disappeared in Mojave Desert. No known family. Frequents Mexican brothels and saloons. Has a few renegade Apache friends both sides of border. Assumed armed and deadly. Have already issued wanted poster for two-hundred-dollar reward DEAD or alive. Will increase reward to five hundred.*

"Look at how the warden capitalized the word *dead,*" Cindy whispered. "It tells me that he sure doesn't ever want to see Cain Hawker back at that prison again."

"Yeah," Longarm agreed, "it's a shame they didn't hang him the minute he was brought to the prison. That would have saved everyone a lot of trouble and expense."

"If he's tied in with renegade Apache," the young detective said, "I doubt they'll ever catch or kill him."

"That's not necessarily so," Longarm argued. "The renegade Apache are being captured, killed, or imprisoned, and there aren't all that many left to raise hell along our southern border. Both the Mexican and American soldiers hunt them relentlessly on both sides of the border. They're a vanishing breed, and so are cold-blooded bastards like Cain Hawker."

"With a two-hundred-dollar reward on his head, I expect someone will betray or kill the man pretty soon," Cindy mused.

"You'd think so," Longarm replied. "That's a fortune down there, but the Apache never betray their own unless they become United States Army scouts because their own families have been killed or harmed by the small and bloody renegade bands."

"So what do we do now?" Cindy asked.

"I'm afraid there isn't much that we can do," Longarm answered. "Maybe we'll get lucky and get a telegram back this week that Hawker has been captured, killed, or hanged. But I won't be holding my breath and waiting for that to happen."

Cindy nodded with understanding. "No, I suppose not. And there is always the chance that the man might just go down deep into Mexico and vanish forever."

"Don't count on it," Longarm said. "Cain Hawker sounds to me like a man who likes blood and money. There isn't any money deep in Mexico unless he goes to work as a hired bodyguard for some rich *patrón* who has enemies. Or for yet another Mexican revolutionary."

"Well, to be truthful," Cindy said, "I hope that I never hear or see the man again. But I have to admit that I doubt that I'll ever get him completely out of my mind."

Longarm understood, and led Cindy outside. "Wait here for a moment, would you?"

"Of course."

Longarm went back into Barstow's office and said to the young detective, "Tell Pete that I want to be kept up to date on Cain Hawker and be told if any word is sent up from Yuma about his death or capture. If anyone tries to collect that two-hundred-dollar reward, I want to know about it right away."

"I'll do that," the detective promised. "And I can tell you that my boss wants to see Cain Hawker brought to justice every bit as much as you do."

"Good," Longarm said, heading back out the door.

"Where are you taking me out to eat tonight?" Cindy asked, linking her arm in his and giving Longarm her most winning smile. "I like my steaks thick, pink, and juicy."

She winked coyly up at him, and it almost made Longarm laugh out loud.

"Glad to hear that," Longarm said.

"You seemed worried inside the detective's office. Does the capture and killing of Cain Hawker mean so much to you?"

"Sure does," Longarm told her. "He almost killed you yesterday morning, and he did kill someone else a few seconds later."

"And he took some gunshots at you," Cindy reminded him.

"Yes. I'm glad he was running hard or he'd have drilled me."

"What a shame that would have been," Cindy said, hugging his arm. "What a loss it would have been for me, too!"

"Glad you think so."

"Oh, I do." Cindy looked up at him. "How long can Pedro and I stay at your rooms?"

"I don't know. Let's just see how it plays out."

"Could be weeks and weeks," Cindy said.

"I should be so lucky."

"We *both* should be so lucky," she countered.

Longarm nodded in agreement, and thought about what a delight this cowgirl from Arizona was turning out to be. But even as he smiled, he was inwardly fretting about what Cain Hawker might be up to, and hoping it didn't have a thing to do with Cindy's small and vulnerable ranching family.

Chapter 7

Longarm, Cindy, and the tomcat named Pedro went back to their respective workday routines for the next month. For Longarm, it was a happy and fun-filled time, and he found to his surprise that Cindy Allison was a woman he could actually stand to live with and be around for extended periods. They attended spring concerts in the city's park, a Shakespearean play, and a circus with clowns, jugglers, a three-legged fat lady, a sword swallower, amazing trapeze artists, and one lumbering elephant named Colossus who crapped prodigious amounts of dung.

Longarm discovered that Cindy had a quick, ribald sense of humor and she was easy to please. The Arizona cowgirl loved to read, and she liked to draw people's faces and horses in all poses. And on top of all that, Cindy was very good at lovemaking and a downright excellent cook. As for the manager where Cindy worked who had been blackmailing her, Longarm paid the U.S. Mint a surprise visit. He knew many of the top officials there, and was well received by them all. So when Bradley happened to see him laughing and joking with Mint Director Hamilton Sebring, the little coward ducked back into his office and hid as if he'd seen a ghost.

"How's it going, Jackrabbit!" Longarm called as he stopped by the man's office grinning like a lunatic. "How's your wiggly little fella hangin' these days?"

Bradley looked as if he were either going to faint or throw himself out the third-story window. His round, fat face was so stricken with fear and embarrassment that Longarm doubled up and burst into laughter, which only made Bradley all the more mortified.

Longarm winked at the bastard. "Best behave yourself, Rabbit, or I'll come back and cut off your little balls!"

Bradley ducked behind his desk and hid until Longarm disappeared with a wide and satisfied grin on his mug, knowing that the man would never, *ever* trouble Cindy Allison again.

Yes, everything was going just fine, and Longarm was even beginning to think that having Cindy and a tomcat in his rooms full-time was a pretty nice way to exist. He had a few local criminal cases that involved federal business, but nothing serious or time-consuming, and so he often just dropped into the office of his boss, Marshal Billy Vail, and shared a cup or two of coffee and the latest local and federal gossip.

"Custis," Billy said, "you seem to be putting on a few pounds these days, and your eyes are never bloodshot anymore in the morning. Don't tell me that you're becoming civilized and sedentary."

"Not a chance," Longarm replied.

"You must have found a woman with more sense

than usual," Billy said, angling for personal and juicy information from the best and by far the most interesting man on his office payroll.

Longarm just shrugged. He didn't like to talk much about his personal life at the office. Over the years, he had already been the source of most of the gossip, and he sure didn't want to add to it now.

But Billy was persistent and inherently nosy. More than that, he was Longarm's boss, and so he could press a little harder with his inquiry. "So what's her name?"

Knowing he had to give his boss some kind of answer, Longarm replied, "She's that young lady that was wounded a while back on the street outside our office."

"Oh, that one!" Billy leaned back in his plush office chair with his fingers laced behind his head. "I heard that she was quite a looker."

"She's a simple Arizona rancher's daughter. A genuine cowgirl."

"Is that a fact?"

"It is."

Billy Vail grinned and waited. Longarm stubbornly kept his silence. Finally, Billy unlaced his fingers and leaned forward. "Want to tell me a little about the lady?"

"Not particularly."

"Bad answer, Custis. Or have you conveniently forgotten that I'm your boss and best friend?"

"You're my boss," Longarm said. "But if you keep prying into my love life, you might not be my best friend much longer."

"My, my!" Billy said expansively, quite obviously enjoying Longarm's discomfort. "We are a little touchy about this one. Could it be . . . could it really be *serious*?"

"Billy, let it alone."

"Not until you tell me a little something about her."

"And why should I do that?"

"Because you'd like another annual pay raise come October, wouldn't you?"

Longarm sighed with resignation. "All right, Boss. The woman is nice to have around. She has a tomcat named Pedro that I've kinda grown to like, and she sketches and laughs a lot and doesn't feel sorry for herself even though she's under a lot of strain."

"What kind of strain?"

"Her family is in real danger of losing their ranch down near Yuma."

Billy just shrugged his round shoulders. "I've been to Yuma and I'd say that losing a piece of real estate down in that hellishly hot part of the country might actually be a blessing."

"Cindy doesn't share that feeling."

"Didn't I read that she was wounded in a random shooting?"

"Yes," Longarm confessed, "but I'm not completely convinced that it *was* random."

Billy's smile evaporated because he sensed something of real importance. "What does that mean?"

In as few words as possible, Longarm explained his fears that Cain Hawker might have actually been trying to kill the woman so that she could not send home money to her desperate ranching family. He ended by saying, "Cindy tells me that the ranch is valuable because it's along the Gila River, so they have plenty of irrigation water and can run a lot of cattle. Unfortunately, due to medical reasons, the family had to sell its herd and there's no money to replace them. No cow herd means no income. Cindy is trying to get her family back on their feet financially. She's got a younger brother who is also a problem and is of no use whatsoever."

"She sounds like the only one in the family who is now capable and responsible."

"That's about the size of it."

"Where does your lady friend work?"

"In the accounting department at the Mint."

"Is she smart and capable, or can you even give me a fair judgment of her abilities outside of your now-happy little home?"

"Cut the crap, Billy!"

"Oh, now I understand," Billy said, leaning back again. "I hit a nerve. Boy, you really must like this one."

"Like I said, I'm fond of her tomcat."

"Sure." Billy laughed. "But is she smart and capable?"

Longarm shrugged. "I don't know. But judging from what I've seen of her, she is no doubt very capable and smart."

"How much are they paying her a month over at the Mint?"

"I think she said forty dollars."

"If she's good with numbers and accounting, I might be able to hire her at sixty."

Longarm sat up straight in his chair. "Dammit, Billy, that's almost what I make after all these years of federal service!"

"Yeah, but you're ugly and I understand that she's not."

Longarm knew that his boss was getting the better of him, and so he clamped his jaw shut tight.

"Custis? Do you want to tell her to come on over here and interview for a promotion?"

"No. She's leaving pretty soon for Arizona."

"How soon?"

"I don't know."

"Well, maybe I can give her enough money to make her change her mind about that. Would that suit you?"

"I guess it wouldn't upset me," Longarm confessed.

"Tell her to come on over and speak to our secretary and set up an interview. Maybe I can help the woman and she can be a real asset to our accounting department, which is floundering and incompetent. The truth of the matter is that people precise with their figures are always damned hard to hire at any salary."

"I'll tell her," Longarm said. "But I'll also tell her what an arrogant boss you can be to work for at times."

"But I'm very honest with my people," Billy said, raising a finger. "Always fair to them and honest."

Longarm nodded because it was truth. For many years, Billy Vail had been, like himself, a deputy marshal in the field, and he had a wall full of framed awards and certificates. He'd been one of the best lawmen in his day, well respected for his ability, bravery, and intelligence, and Longarm appreciated the fact that Billy never bragged or boasted about his sterling field career. The truth of the matter was that they liked and respected each other. And if Billy would just stop putting his nose into Longarm's love life, then the relationship between them would have been damn near perfect.

Cindy Allison was excited about possibly working for the United States marshal's office in the Federal Building. She had heard from the start that it was a great place to work, and when she learned that she might actually be employed in the same department as Longarm, she thought that was the icing on the cake.

"How do I look?" she asked nervously, smoothing her dress and hair on the morning before the interview.

"You look sexy and gorgeous," Longarm told her with a smile.

"Gorgeous is all right, sexy isn't. After all, you did tell me that Mr. Vail is a married man with children."

"That's right. He's a good, faithful husband and loving father, but that doesn't mean he doesn't have eyes and a fairly lusty imagination."

Cindy frowned. "Well, I hope that isn't what he's thinking when he interviews me. I want to be hired on my ability, not my looks."

"Sorry, darlin', but you can't have one without the other."

"I sure hope that I get the job. Did he really say that he might be able to start me at sixty dollars a month?"

"Something like that," Longarm mumbled, still a little annoyed that she might be getting close to what he earned even though he'd been employed there for several years.

Cindy took in a deep breath. "If I could make that much money, I could certainly send the additional dollars to my family and it would help them immensely."

"Just relax and be yourself and I'm sure that you'll be hired," Longarm told her.

"And he wouldn't be doing it just for my looks or because of us?"

"Nope. Billy may tease and joke, but when it comes to spending his department's money, he expects value. If he doesn't think you can earn your salary, he won't hire you."

"Fair enough," Cindy said, looking satisfied with the answer. "Wish me luck this morning."

"I wish you luck," Longarm said with a smile.

"If I get the job and pay raise, I'll take you out to the best restaurant in town tonight."

"Deal!"

Cindy rushed out the door and Longarm went over to Pedro. "That's a good woman you got there. I hope she gets the job."

Pedro began to purr. He was a loving tomcat and no fuss in the rooms, even if he was completely useless and shed a hell of a lot of hair.

Chapter 8

"Custis! I got the job!" Cindy cried that May afternoon when she showed up carrying a new purse and wearing a badly needed new dress and a new pair of fashionable shoes. "And Mr. Vail is starting me out at fifty-seven dollars a week, with a raise to sixty after a month of satisfactory performance."

Longarm was relaxing on his old sofa, petting Pedro the yellow cat, when she burst in the door. He dropped the cat, took Cindy up in his arms, and swung her around the room. "Congratulations! I was sure that once you had that interview, Billy . . . I mean Mr. Vail . . . would hire you. When do you start?"

"Monday."

"Today is Thursday and we'll celebrate all weekend. We'll go out and do the town in grand style."

"But I want to pay for it this time, and I don't have any extra money yet," Cindy told him with a frown. "I did have a little, but I really needed to buy this new dress and these shoes. I can't be making all that money and show up in your accounting department looking like a beggar woman, now can I?"

"Nope," he said. "And don't worry about the money. If you really want us to go out on your treat, then I'll advance you twenty dollars. But there are strings attached to the offer."

"Strings?"

"Yes. Instead of interest on the twenty, I expect very personal *services*."

She arched her eyebrows. "What kind of 'services' were you thinking about, Marshal Long?"

"I'm sure you can guess."

Cindy laughed and gave him a kiss. "All right! Deal!"

Longarm took Cindy's new purse from her hand and led her into his bedroom. He began fondling and kissing her until she protested. "We're going to wrinkle up this new dress and . . ."

But Longarm didn't let her finish. He kissed her mouth passionately, then undressed and mounted her like a stallion. "Twenty dollars in services paid two dollars a poke."

"Two dollars!" she cried in mock outrage. "Is that all my poor body is worth to you? A paltry two dollars a poke!"

"No," he confessed, driving his thick rod into her honey pot, "but I'm trying to drive a *hard* bargain."

"What you're driving is hard, but it's sure not a bargain," she moaned as she wrapped her legs around his waist and joined him in an energetic and happy bout of frenzied lovemaking.

The next morning, Cindy was at work enjoying her last day at the United States Mint when Longarm showed up unexpectedly. Cindy jumped up from her desk chair with surprise and came to him with a smile, until she saw the serious look on his face. "Custis? Is something wrong?"

"I'm afraid so," he told her in a low voice. "I stopped by Detective Barstow's office and there was a telegram from Yuma."

"From the warden at the prison?"

"No," he said, taking Cindy's arm and leading her away from the other employees, who were gawking and eavesdropping. "It was from the marshal down in Yuma. I'd sent him a telegram about you and your family's situation."

"What?" Cindy shook her head with obvious confusion. "You're not making sense, Custis. Why would you tell a marshal about me and my family's problems?"

"More than anything, I was concerned about their safety," he said, leading her into an office.

"Excuse me!" a very well dressed department manager said with annoyance.

"Excuse us," Longarm told the startled manager. "But I need a moment of privacy here. Could you leave us alone for a few minutes?"

The man threw up his hands in exasperation "But . . . but this is my personal office!"

Longarm was not in the mood to explain to this bureaucrat what was so important right now. So he simply moved around the fellow's desk, grabbed his arm, and yanked him out of his chair. "It'll only be a few minutes, and I'm sorry about this intrusion, but I really do need a few private moments with Miss Allison *right now*."

The department manager was upset and confused, but

Longarm's strong and forceful manner left no doubt that he was leaving his own office. So, trying to look in control, he quickly decided it would be better to cooperate with the big man than to struggle and look like a weakling in front of his fellow government workers.

"Of course," he stammered as Longarm shoved him out the door and began to firmly close it behind him. "But only for a few minutes, because I have a lot of work to do today. A lot of very important work."

"Sure you do," Longarm agreed, turning back to Cindy.

"What is going on here?" she demanded. "This is my last day of work, and I sure don't want to leave it looking like a ninny or a fool. If you have some wild fantasy about screwing me on this government desk, then this is definitely not the time or the place to make that fantasy come true. Maybe this weekend, on *your* desk, we can—"

"Cindy," Longarm interrupted, "please sit down. I have something very bad to tell you."

She had been about to say something, but his words froze her and she blinked. "Custis?"

He gently escorted her to the seat that had just been vacated. "Cindy, I have some terrible news. Maybe I should have waited until you came to our rooms after work, but I just couldn't wait because we need to take immediate action."

Confusion and fear flooded into her blue eyes. "What are you . . ."

Longarm didn't know how to put this in a gentle way to ease her pain, so he simply said, "Your mother and father were found yesterday, murdered at your ranch."

Cindy's jaw dropped and her head began to shake back and forth in silent disbelief and stubborn denial.

"It's true," Longarm whispered. "And your brother, Monty, was beaten almost to death in your ranch house. The telegram said that he is fighting for his life and it's not known whether he will survive."

"No!" she cried. "This is impossible! I'm having a nightmare."

"I'm afraid that it's not impossible," Longarm said, kneeling at her side. "I got the telegram less than an hour ago from Yuma. It's very brief, but there is no mistaking that your family has been attacked and your parents brutally murdered."

Cindy's breath exploded and she howled in torment. "No! No! No!"

Longarm enveloped her in his powerful arms and let her sob out her anguish. He simply didn't have any words to express how sorry he was for the girl and this sudden and unspeakable tragedy. Cindy had told him often how much she loved her father and mother and how much she worried about her wild and irresponsible younger brother, Monty. Now, the elder two were dead and her sixteen-year-old brother was fighting for his life.

The ousted office manager opened the door and peeked inside. Longarm shot him a look that made the man retreat and close the door again. Longarm held Cindy tight until everyone was finally gone for the day and the office was empty. Then, supporting her and with her head against his shoulder, he helped Cindy out of the Mint.

"I've got to go home to Arizona now," Cindy whispered after they were back in Longarm's rooms. "I can't stay here in Denver any longer, even though everything was turning my way."

"I expected you to say that."

She wasn't listening to Longarm, and continued. "Monty isn't a good brother, but he didn't deserve this and I've always felt that he had promise. That he was basically a good kid. He just fell in with some wild friends and went astray for a while. Now, I'm all the family he has left and he's all that I've got left."

"No," Longarm countered, "you've got me and Pedro."

She tried to smile at his lame attempt to comfort and humor her, but she failed badly. Even so, he could see that she was collecting herself and mentally deciding what she should do next for Monty and her ranch.

"Custis, I really, really care for you. But I have to go back to Arizona on the first train or stagecoach. Will you tell Mr. Vail that I'm very sorry that I can't go to work for him on Monday morning?"

"I'll write him a note," Longarm promised. "I'll put it on his desk with a short explanation. He'll hold the job for you, Cindy. If you ever want to come back here to Denver, you'll have that accounting job."

She swallowed hard. "I don't think I can ever come back. I just . . . I just don't know anything right now except that my mother and father have been murdered. I have to go home."

"You will, but not alone," he vowed. "I've got plenty of saved-up vacation time, and Billy will give me extra time away from work if it's needed."

She looked up through her red and teary eyes and

studied his face. "Are you saying that you're coming with me?'

"Yes. That's exactly what I'm saying."

"Oh, Custis!" She threw her arms around him and wept bitterly. "I can't thank you enough!"

"We have to find a temporary home for good Pedro and make travel arrangements. He's a special cat and I'm going to say that we want him back."

"I'm not coming back," she said. "Not if I can save my brother and our ranch."

"All right, then *I'll* take him back. We've become friends. We like and understand each other and he seems happy here in my rooms."

"He is. And so was I."

"Maybe you'll change your mind about returning," Longarm said hopefully. "At any rate, I'll purchase tickets for two on the Denver and Rio Grande for tomorrow morning's departure. If all goes well, we'll be in Pueblo tomorrow and in Yuma a week later."

"It took me almost two weeks to get here from home."

"I'm sure that it did," Longarm told her. "But I travel often and I know ways to get to Arizona fast. I also know all the conductors and people who own the stage-coach lines. Trust me, Cindy. I'll get us to Yuma as fast as is humanly possible."

"You're going to help find out who killed them." It was a statement rather than a question.

"Yes," he replied in a voice that was hard and determined. "And I'm sure that your brother will be able to identify the killer or killers."

"If Monty lives." A tear slid down her cheeks.

"That's right," Longarm agreed. "If your brother lives. But even if he doesn't, I do have an idea who might have been the attacker."

Without a moment's hesitation, she said, "Cain Hawker."

"Yes. And it makes sense. Hawker must have been hired to come here and put a stop to you sending money to your family. That way, they would lose the ranch. When he failed and I caused him to have to flee Denver with a bullet wound, he went after your family. Different target, same result."

"The loss of my family ranch."

"Exactly."

Cindy hugged Longarm and cried. Cried and cried until Pedro came over and rubbed his sleek, fat, and furry body against them both as if understanding their pain and trying to offer whatever he could in the way of support and comfort.

Yeah, Longarm thought, even if Cindy Allison was about to exit his life and his rooms, he'd have her Pedro when he returned from Arizona.

Chapter 9

Longarm and Cindy Allison rode the Southern Pacific Railroad from Tucson to Yuma, and arrived on May 17, when the afternoon temperature was already pegged at over one hundred fiery degrees. In the deepest part of summer, this country would reach temperatures of over 120 degrees in the shade, and neither man nor beast would be able to do much of anything in the afternoon sun.

Longarm knew that some ten years earlier, the town had been called Arizona City, but it was renamed Yuma and was now the county seat. Gazing out the window of the train as it pulled into the desert town, Longarm could see the Yuma Territorial Prison perched on a sunbaked and treeless bluff that overlooked both the Gila and the Colorado Rivers. The town itself had expanded significantly in the five years since he'd visited this part of southern Arizona, but at first glance, its appearance sure hadn't. As far as Longarm could tell, this was still a poor, hot, and dusty community whose main support was from the territorial prison, the Colorado River trade, and agriculture.

"What's growing in those irrigated fields?" Longarm asked, pointing to the south and east.

"Cotton," Cindy replied. "Cotton, corn, and alfalfa are our main crops. Some of it is barged down to the Sea of Cortez and on to other distant ports, but a lot of it we use right here for cattle feed and for manufacturing clothes. Mexico buys some of the cotton, and the rest is shipped to the mills in California."

Longarm shook his head. "The Yuma Territorial Prison looks as hard and ugly as I remembered."

"Is any prison supposed to look appealing?"

"No," Longarm admitted, "but this one always struck me as looking about as bad as a prison could possibly look. I'd think that new convicts coming here would pretty much lose heart the moment they set eyes on it."

"Yes," she agreed. "Not many even attempt to escape. And those that do often drown in the swift currents of the Colorado River, die of thirst in the surrounding deserts, or end up being tortured and killed by the Apache. That's why so few even try."

"Cain Hawker did."

"Yes, I know," Cindy replied. "And even he would have died if he had not been found and saved by his friends among the renegade Apache. And as for the prison itself, I'm betting that it will stand on that barren bluff forever."

Custis nodded with grim agreement. The prison, with its somber sandstone guard towers and rock and adobe buildings, looked as if it would easily defy both man and nature for centuries.

Cindy touched his arm. "Have you ever been inside of the prison?"

"As a matter of fact, I have," Longarm said. "It's a depressing hellhole. I wouldn't put a dog in those little cavelike cells they have for the inmates, many of whom die from the heat, or just commit suicide rather than endure their full prison sentences."

"So I've heard. They have a cemetery up there on the bluff, and I'm told that each month they add one or two more graves."

"For my money," Longarm said, his mouth forming a hard, unforgiving line, "Cain Hawker should be in one of them."

Cindy, perhaps wanting to change the subjected, pointed and said, "That's our ranch out there with the adobe house under all those big cottonwood trees. My father planted those trees the first year he took title to the land."

"How long ago was that?"

"More than forty years. Father and Mother homesteaded it when the Apache and Yuma Indians were still raiding all over this part of southern Arizona. There has been bloodshed and fighting between the Anglos and the Yuma and Apache in this low desert for centuries. In 1780, the Spaniards established settlements along both the Gila and Colorado Rivers. Missionaries, soldiers, and settlers moved here, but the soldiers were cruel and oppressive to the local Yuma Indians. The Yuma were farmers, and I've been told that the Spanish soldiers would wait until the Indians harvested their crops each fall, and then they would raid their storehouses, rape their women, and get drunk on fiery tequila and liquor they made from the stolen corn harvest."

"So there was a bloody Indian uprising," Longarm said, knowing that would be the inevitable result of the Spanish soldiers plundering.

"Yes," Cindy replied. "One blistering day in July of 1781, the Yuma decided to forever rid themselves of their Spanish oppressors. During two awful days, they slaughtered four Franciscan friars, more than thirty Spanish soldiers, and almost that many white settlers who had claimed the best Indian farmlands along the two rivers. The graves of those dead are now overgrown by creosote and sagebrush, their names and histories all forgotten. Some of the Spanish farmers had women and children who also were slaughtered."

Longarm nodded. "So then the land went back to the Yuma and Apache after the massacre in 1781?"

"It did," Cindy answered. "For many, many years, the Indians would kill all white people who entered this part of the country. They did that until gold was discovered in California nearly seventy years later and hordes of white prospectors began to pour across Yuma lands in numbers too large for the Indians to exterminate. After that, the Yuma and their neighbors the Apache were the ones being wiped out. Today, there aren't many Yuma who have survived the white man's diseases and white man's revenge. The ones remaining eke out their bare existence on a small reservation and face an unending and wretched future."

Longarm understood what Cindy was telling him. Most American Indian tribes, whether they were up in the vast, grassy Northern Plains or in the harsh, dry

Southwest, had similar histories of initial resistance, then disease and conquest, inevitably resulting in a hard, poverty-stricken reservation life. Only the fierce and unyielding Apache still roamed free, and even they were traveling in small, desperate raiding bands. And in just such a band, Longarm figured he might find the murdering red-haired Cain Hawker.

When the train pulled up at the station in Yuma, Longarm and Cindy disembarked and were met by a local lawman who introduced himself as Marshal Tom Beason. He was a handsome young man who stood about six feet tall, with sandy hair and an open, friendly smile. But Longarm noticed that Beason walked with a pronounced limp and his lean body was cocked just a mite to the left. Beason extended his hand and his grip was strong. Longarm sized him up as a good and capable lawman, although perhaps a greenhorn, a man short on experience in going after and apprehending outlaws and renegade Indians.

"You'd be Deputy United States Marshal Custis Long." Beason removed his battered Stetson hat and placed it on his chest. With a slight bow, he said, turning to the woman at Longarm's side, "And you would be Miss Cindy Allison. Miss Allison, I'm awful darn sorry to have had to send that telegram to Denver about the death of your family."

Cindy nodded, fighting off tears and unable to speak.

Needing to change the subject, Longarm said, "Marshal Beason, I'm surprised that, in a town of this small size, you haven't previously met Miss Allison."

"I was only recently assigned to Yuma and this part of the Arizona Territory," Beason explained.

"Did you do something really bad to get sent down here?"

"Nope," Tom Beason answered. "I *asked* to be assigned here in southern Arizona."

When Longarm cocked an eyebrow and regarded the younger man with obvious skepticism, Beason explained, "I was a top bronc buster for ten years up in Montana. Over time, the broncs got to busting me a little too often, and the bitterly long and cold Montana winters made my accumulation of broken bones ache like the devil. So I decided I needed a warmer climate and a new line of work."

"I guess there's some sense to be made of that," Longarm conceded, "but living in Yuma and being a town marshal could also prove very bad for your health."

"I'll take my chances here," Beason said with a confident smile. "I like the heat and I don't ache anymore. And there are things about the desert that are downright beautiful."

Longarm pivoted around in a full circle, with his eyes scanning the dust and shimmering heat waves that undulated across the ugly sage desert and alkali flats. He had a feeling he might actually be missing something. "Oh, yeah? Like what, Tom?"

"The sunsets and the sunrises," Beason told him without a moment's hesitation. "They are the most beautiful I've ever seen. And at night, it's always warm enough to sit on a porch swing and study the stars. Some nights, I've counted more than a dozen shooters, and most of 'em looked so close to me that, if had I been quick enough, I could have snatched 'em out of the sky with my bare hands."

"Hmmm," Longarm mused. "I never really thought about that kind of entertainment."

"Well, it's nice and it don't cost a man a thing to count shooting stars," Beason gushed. "And I love to fish. Down here, you can fish year-round in both the Gila and the Colorado Rivers. Trout. Bass. Catfish. They grow some monsters in these warm rivers."

"Do say?"

"That's right," Beason assured him. He winked and said, "Now, Marshal Long, you're from Denver. Can you fish from November to March in that high, cold country?"

Before Longarm could even reply, Beason answered his own obvious question. "Of course you can't! You'd freeze, or be so cold that you wouldn't want to fish."

"Marshal Beason," Cindy said, "I'm sure that we both appreciate your love of this desert country. I happen to share that same love, and I also used to count shooting stars as they blazed across the heavens. But—"

"You did?" The lawman's handsome face split into a wide grin. "Well, for goodness sakes alive! I'm sure glad to hear that, Miss Allison. Some people think I'm sun-stroked when I tell 'em I like to count stars, but now seeing you and knowin' you sure ain't touched by the heat and sun makes me feel just a whole lot better."

Longarm removed his hat and wiped sweat from his forehead. "Marshal, all this talk of shooting stars is really interesting, but we've got two murders on our hands and we need to get down to serious law business."

"Of course we do." Beason looked ashamed of himself. "I'm sorry to have got off on the wrong foot."

Cindy asked, "Where are my parents right now?"

"Buried real nice in our cemetery," Beason answered, pointing off toward the cemetery on a low, sun-blasted hill lacking either grass or shade. "In this heat, we just couldn't keep 'em until you arrived. I hope you understand. They got a real fine and dignified burial and service, Miss Allison. Some of your neighbors chipped in and helped pay for the caskets, flowers, and the like. Of course, we don't have much in the way of flowers in this hot season, but we picked a few wild ones that were down along the riverbanks. And everything about laying your parents to their final rest was all done nice and Christian proper."

"I'll visit them at sundown," Cindy decided in a voice that trembled. "When it's cooler. And I very much appreciate what you've done, Marshal Beason."

He swept his hat off again and did that little bow. "Call me Tom, miss. Just plain old Tom. And if there is anything at all that I can do for you just let me know."

For some reason, Beason was starting to grate a little on Longarm. He was just being too damn nice, and Longarm was thinking that Tom Beason was smitten with Cindy.

"What about my brother?" she asked.

Marshal Beason's face split into a grin. "I was just about to tell you about him, Miss Allison. I saw your brother less than an hour ago, and I'm real happy to tell you that he's on the road to a complete recovery."

Cindy instinctively reached out and grasped the young Yuma lawman's arm. "Thank you!"

Beason blushed and shuffled his feet. "Oh, I didn't have anything to do with it. Doc Potter and his wife took your brother into their home, and they nursed him night and day the first week after he was beaten. Monty was in real bad shape when we found him. I don't know how he lived through that beating, but he did and he's on the mend and staying in our best hotel."

"I want to go see him right now," Cindy said.

"Me, too," Longarm added. "Did he give you a description of the man or men who attacked him and killed his parents?"

"He did for a fact, and it was just like your telegram said, Marshal Long. It was the red-haired escaped convict named Cain Hawker."

"Have you gone after the man?"

"No, but there is a two-hundred-dollar reward for Hawker . . . dead or alive. That kind of money is unheard of down here, and someone will sure enough set out to claim it. I have heard that a few men joined up and are searching for Hawker right this very minute. I'm fully expecting that they'll be bringing him into Yuma most likely tied across his saddle, head down, and deader than a tromped horned toad."

"Let's go see Monty," Cindy urged, picking up her bag from the train station and then starting off toward town.

Tom Beason fell in beside Longarm for a moment and whispered, "Her kid brother is . . . well, he's troubled."

"How so?" Longarm asked.

"He's bitter and he's hurt. Young Monty Allison has been through hell, and he's taking the murders of his parents real hard."

"I can understand that," Longarm said.

"He's got some healing to do, Marshal Long. He's a good-lookin' kid, but this Cain Hawker must have put the boot to him when he was down and unconscious. Monty has busted ribs and a cracked skull."

"Given what I've seen and heard about Cain Hawker, the boy is damned fortunate even to be alive," Longarm said.

"That's true enough."

"Is he talking?"

"Not much."

"I'll want to interview him," Longarm said.

"I figured you would. From what I can gather, Monty Allison was a wild kid and headed for trouble even before this happened to his poor family. Now, well, I just don't know how it's gonna affect him in the head . . . but it can't be for the better."

Longarm understood. "Sometimes, almost dying can make a person think about life and how they've got to take hold and better themselves."

Beason looked skeptical. "You think that might happen to young Monty Allison?"

"I've seen good things like that come out of bad things quite a few times," Longarm assured the lawman. "But only some time will tell how Monty Allison comes out."

"I'm awful glad that you decided to come here with Miss Allison," Tom Beason confided. "She's gonna need a lot of support and protection."

Longarm could understand this greenhorn using the word "support," but he wasn't sure why he'd also used the word "protection." But Longarm would find out soon enough. He'd protect Cindy Allison and he'd make sure that Cain Hawker was dragged kicking and screaming to a Yuma hanging tree with or without the help of bounty hunters.

Chapter 10

"Monty was just moved a few hours ago from Doc Potter's place over to the Rawhide Hotel where the doctor can easily check up on him three or four times a day," Beason told them as they hurried down the street.

"Have you visited him yet?" Longarm asked.

"I have," Beason answered, "but he didn't want to talk. The kid just described Cain Hawker to me and then turned his head away. From what I've heard, Monty Allison is not the least bit sociable."

"He's been badly beaten and our parents were murdered," Cindy snapped in her brother's defense. "So I don't see how you can blame Monty for being unfriendly."

"Miss, I'm not blaming your brother for anything," Beason countered. "I sure didn't mean it to sound that way either. Given what your brother has been through, I reckon anyone would be bitter and upset."

They arrived at the Rawhide Hotel and Beason said, "I knew you were coming so I took the liberty of booking you a couple of hotel rooms. Marshal Long, your room is on the first floor, Number four, and Miss Allison is on the second floor, Room Twenty-one, which is right next to her brother."

"Thank you," Cindy told the young lawman as they swept inside the hotel, not even bothering to take in the nice lobby with its polished floor and dark walnut wood paneling.

"Custis," Cindy said, "I'd appreciate it if you'd give me a few minutes alone with Monty before you go up and question him."

"Of course," Longarm agreed. "I'll dump my things in my room and be out here waiting in the lobby when you come down."

When Cindy climbed up the stairs to the second floor, Longarm went to the registration desk, registered, and got his room key. A few moments later, with Marshal Beason still in tow, he put his things in his room, then went back outside and looked around at the hotel lobby. "This will do fine, although I'm not expecting to be here for much of my stay."

Tom Beason asked, "How long *will* you be here, Marshal?"

"I have no idea," Longarm told the local lawman. "I guess that all depends on how long it will take to arrest or kill Cain Hawker."

"That could take quite a while. Maybe you should just let the bounty hunters do the job and go back to Denver. I'll send you telegrams and keep you updated."

"I appreciate your cooperation," Longarm said, "but I've never had a lot of faith in bounty hunters."

"Why not?"

"Because most of them are amateurs," Longarm said

with his usual bluntness. "They're farmers or cowboys or ex-soldiers who think that bringing a man in for his bounty will be quick and easy work. Oftentimes, it is. However, I have a feeling that Cain Hawker is going to be very, very difficult to bring to justice because of his association with renegade Apache."

"I'd have to agree with you under ordinary circumstances," Beason said. "But Hawker has a two-hundred-dollar reward on his head, and that's one hell of a lot of money. Sure, the amateurs will try to collect the bounty, but so will the best of the professionals. I've heard that several of them are already on Hawker's trail."

"A trail that will probably lead them into Mexico," Longarm told the man. "And down there, you never know what will happen. If they run into the Mexican authorities before Hawker, they could be arrested. And if the Mexican authorities learn of the two-hundred-dollar bounty, they'll want a big piece of that for themselves."

Beason could not hide his surprise. "They will?"

"Oh, yes," Longarm said. "Every officer within a hundred miles of Cain Hawker will suddenly drop what they are doing and hunt for Hawker."

"Isn't that good?"

"It might be," Longarm said, "except that, if Cain Hawker can pay the Mexicans more than he's worth to us dead or alive, then they'll take his money and let him go free."

"They'd really do that?"

"In a heartbeat," Longarm assured Beason. "And if some bounty hunter gets in the way of their making money . . . that bounty hunter will just disappear."

Beason frowned and rubbed his chin. "I've never been down in Mexico, and for sure not on official business. I've heard nothing but bad things can happen down there to a gringo who carries a badge."

"You're dead right about that," Longarm told the lawman. "If Hawker's trail leads me south of the border, then I leave my badge and authority right here in Yuma."

"But you're a *federal* marshal," Beason said with confusion.

"They hate federal officers even worse than local ones like you," Longarm explained. "What would you do if some Mexican official came up here to Yuma and started messing in your affairs?"

"I see your point," Beason conceded. "I'd resent the interference."

"Just as they do," Longarm replied. He sank down on a soft velvet sofa and rested his heels on a coffee table littered with old newspapers and magazines. Longarm was tired. It had been a hard trip covering a lot of miles in a big hurry, and what he really needed was some good food and a good night's sleep in a real feather bed.

"You look exhausted," Beason said. "It was probably a difficult trip coming all the way out here."

"It was," Longarm confessed. "But I'm not complaining and neither is Cindy. She needed to get here fast, and I'm just hoping that her kid brother won't turn out to be a lot of trouble. Cindy already has troubles enough."

"You'd be referring to the death of her parents."

"Yes, and the financial situation concerning her ranch."

"She's having money problems on top of everything else?" Beason asked with genuine concern.

"It's not my place to tell you about her troubles," Longarm began, "but since I think it is relevant to the murders, then I suppose I'm not overstepping my personal and professional bounds."

In the next few minutes, Longarm told Beason his theory regarding why Cindy Allison had been attacked by Cain Hawker on the streets of Denver, and how her family had been forced into dire financial circumstances because of the failing health of her parents and the legal fees required to represent Monty Allison in court.

"Yeah," Beason said, "I knew about the kid being in trouble and having to have an expensive attorney to keep him out of the Yuma Prison. It was big news here in Yuma not long ago. It's a shame that Miss Allison has to deal with a brother like that on top of all her other troubles. It's remarkable that she's standing up to the pressure as well as she is."

"She's a remarkable woman," Longarm replied. "She was doing very well in Denver, and was sending money back here to help her parents keep their ranch when the news of their death came."

"Some people get more than their share of grief in this world."

"Have you had a lot of grief in your life, Tom?"

The young man shrugged his broad shoulders. "I had a rotten childhood, but so have many others. My father abandoned my mother when I was three years old, so I never knew him. My mother moved in with my grand folks and they were good to us, but Grandpa was always sorta crotchety. I think he resented having to help support his daughter and grandson. At any rate, I left them when I was fourteen and went to work on a cattle ranch. By the time I was eighteen, I was a top hand drawing top wages."

"Have you done a lot of hunting?"

"You mean for deer and other wild game?" Beason asked.

"That's right."

"No. But why are you asking me that question?"

Longarm replied, "Tom, have you ever *killed* a man before?"

Beason blinked with surprise and maybe shock. He swallowed hard and said, "I have not."

"How good are you with a gun?"

"Passable."

Longarm shook his head. "I mean no offense, Tom, but 'passable' isn't going to take you to a rocking chair and old age in this profession. There are a lot of men who break the law and are far more than 'passable' with a gun or a rifle."

"I'll practice some. And I know how to use a shotgun. Doesn't take much practice to hit what you're aiming for with one of them."

"Practice a lot with your rifle and pistol," Longarm urged. "Look, Tom, I'm not here to make you look inferior or give you a bad time, but—"

"But what?" Tom Beason demanded with irritation. "If you've got something to say about me, then spit it out."

"All right, I will," Longarm told him after reaching a hard decision. "What I want to say is that most successful and long-lived lawmen come from troubled backgrounds and hard fights. Many are Civil War veterans who faced other men on the bloody battlefields time after time. But even those who have never shot another man before almost always came from hunting backgrounds. They are boys who grew into manhood hunting and tracking game. And, Tom, you don't seem to have done a lot of either."

Tom Beason looked away for a moment as if to gather his thoughts. "Marshal, I'm going to assume that you have my best interests at heart. That you're concerned about my health in this profession. And for that, I say thank you. But what you don't know about me is that I am tough, honest, and brave enough to stand up to a man in the street or in a saloon and either back him down or arrest him."

"But how can you do that if he's better with a gun and kills or wounds you, Tom?"

"I . . . I don't know the answer to that one."

"You should start asking yourself that question," Longarm said, "because a man like Cain Hawker will show you no mercy, and he's good with both a gun and his huge fists."

"I've been in plenty of fistfights," Beason said defensively. "And I've always held my own . . . even against bigger men."

"I'm not surprised to hear that," Longarm told the younger man. "Have you ever had to fight an Apache?"

"No."

"I have," Longarm said. "I've got the scars to prove it. They don't fight like a white man. They fight with knives and teeth. They scratch, claw, and go for your eyes and balls. They're like wildcats."

Tom Beason had taken a seat beside Longarm on the couch, but now he came to his feet and looked down at Custis, saying, "You're as much as telling me that I'll lose a fight against an Apache or tough outlaw."

"Not only lose the fight," Longarm told him, "but most likely lose your life."

"I'm not quitting this line of work," Tom said stubbornly as he laced his strong arms across his chest. "And I'm not going to sit on my butt while you go chasing after Hawker. I'm coming along to help you bring him to justice."

"You can't," Longarm told him. "The locals depend upon you for protection, and I'm most likely leaving town tomorrow. I will probably go down in Mexico to track Hawker down. Do you really think that the people of Yuma are going to give you the time off to go on a manhunt?"

There was a long pause. "No, I guess not."

"Then you'll stay here, and I want you to keep your ear to the ground and see if you can hear anything about Hawker that might prove useful."

"Such as?"

"I believe that someone hired him to kill Cindy's parents as well as Cindy earlier in Denver. I want you to see if you can find out who would want to do that and have the money to pay Hawker."

"I'll see what I can do."

"Also," Longarm said, "keep a close eye on both Cindy and her kid brother."

Beason's face showed his sudden concern. "Do you think their lives could still be in danger?"

"I don't know. But whoever hired Cain Hawker

might just decide to hire someone else to finish the job. We just can't take any chances."

"I'll watch them like a hawk," Tom Beason promised. "I sure hope that you find Hawker fast . . . or some of those bounty hunters catch and then kill him quick."

"If one of them kills Hawker, then we'd never know who hired him in the first place," Longarm explained. "And that's what we have to find out. Otherwise, we could just have another man trying to finish the job Hawker didn't quite complete."

"Yeah, you're right," Beason said, nodding his head with understanding. "Anything else I can do to help while I wait here in Yuma?"

"Yes," Longarm said. "I was serious when I said that you need to practice with both your gun and your rifle. Practice at least an hour a day."

"That's a lot of time and I'm pretty busy."

"Find the time, even if you have to get up before dawn and ride a ways out of town to do the shooting."

Beason nodded with acceptance.

"Anything else?"

Longarm shook his head, and just then he saw Cindy coming down the hotel room's second floor. There were tears on her cheeks, and Longarm figured that meant Cindy's reunion with her troubled kid brother had not gone at all well.

Chapter 11

Longarm mounted the hotel's creaking stairs and knocked on Monty Allison's door.

"Go away!" came a hoarse shout.

Longarm ignored the kid, opened his unlocked door, and stepped into the room. Inside the small, hot room, the faded curtains were drawn and the light was poor, but even so, Longarm could see that Monty's head and half of his face were swathed in bandages. When Longarm opened the curtains a few inches, he could see that the Allison kid's lips and neck were purple, and it was clear that he had taken a near-fatal beating in addition to nearly being strangled.

"Monty, I'm Deputy United States Marshal Custis Long, and I really need to talk to you."

"I got nothin' to say," the kid said, broken lips twisting downward at the corners. "Marshal, get the hell out of my room."

"Not until we have a talk," Longarm said, taking a chair beside the young man and removing his own flat-brimmed Stetson. "I want to hear exactly what happened at your ranch."

"I already went over that with Marshal Beason. Ask him to tell you about it."

"I need to hear it from you," Longarm said, noting that Monty Allison was a tall, slender kid who showed the promise of becoming a big and good looking man. But you could tell that he was hardened beyond his years and hated authority, which was the reason he had nearly gotten himself sent to prison. "All right, Monty, tell me right from the start everything that happened when Cain Hawker showed up at your ranch house and killed your folks."

"Why should I!" Monty spat, dark eyes burning with anger. "I've already told the story once, and then again just now to my sister. I'm sick and tired of going over it."

"I don't care how sick and tired you are," Longarm replied, leaning closer toward the kid and staring into those angry eyes. "I have to hear it with my own ears."

"I'm not in the mood to talk right now, so leave."

"Listen," Longarm said, trying to be patient. "The sooner you get started telling me the details, then the sooner I'll be able to leave and go after Hawker and bring him in dead or alive."

"I'm going to settle the score with that sonofabitch."

Longarm pretended not to have heard that remark. "Monty, I'm sure that your sister told you that Cain Hawker also tried to kill her on the streets of Denver."

"Yeah, she told me that. But why would he go clear to Colorado to kill my sister?"

"I believe that Cain Hawker was hired by someone

with money who lives around here, and that man desperately wants the title to your ranch."

"There are lots of ranches for sale around here, and ours isn't all that special. Why the hell would Hawker go to so much trouble to get our Double A Ranch?"

"Because it's on the Gila River and that means it will always have water. My guess is that the water rights to the Double A are worth even more than the land. So my first question is, do you have any idea who might want your family's ranch land and water rights?"

"No."

"Think!" Longarm demanded in a hard voice. "You've been around these parts for sixteen years and you have a good pair of eyes and ears. Has anyone recently offered to buy your parents out?"

"Maybe."

Longarm wanted to slap the kid, but that would be unconscionable, so he controlled his temper and managed to say, "What the hell does 'maybe' mean?"

Monty Allison sighed with feigned boredom. "All right. Mr. Caldwell at the Bank of Yuma has been trying to get my folks to sell the ranch to him and his assistant."

"Why?"

"Because he holds the note to the Double A on a loan he made to my parents about two years ago."

"Do you know how much the note is worth?"

"Almost two hundred dollars."

"That's a lot of money," Longarm said.

"More than my folks could ever have come up with," Monty said. "But I was there when Mr. Caldwell told my parents that, if they didn't sell to him and his partner, they were going to foreclose on the note. That would mean that my family would lose the ranch to bankruptcy, and we'd wind up with little or no money to show for all our years of hard work."

"Was anyone with Mr. Caldwell in that room when that conversation took place?"

"His assistant and partner at the bank, Mr. Bob Roach."

"And what did your parents say to Mr. Caldwell and Mr. Roach after they warned them that your ranch would be sold in bankruptcy?"

Monty managed a cold smile. "My old man told those bankers to go screw themselves. Yep. That's exactly what he told them. He said that Cindy was making a lot of money in Denver and that she was sending most of it to him to pay off the debts and restock our cattle herd."

Longarm saw that all the pieces were falling into place now. "And what kind of response did that bring from the two bankers?"

"They scoffed at the old man and told him that my sister couldn't possibly send enough money to eliminate the debt and save our ranch. Then, Mr. Caldwell upped the price he said he was willing to pay for the Double A. He said it was his last and best offer for our ranch."

"And your father's response?"

Monty gave a cold laugh. "The old man told both bankers they could shove a broom handle up their high-and-mighty asses and fly their brooms right out the door!"

Longarm glanced away for a moment with his mind churning.

"Marshal Long?"

"Yeah?"

"You don't think that those bankers had anything to do with that red-haired giant that murdered my parents and beat me until he thought I was almost dead, do you?"

"As a matter of fact, I think that they might have had *everything* to do with it," Longarm answered. "It just makes perfect sense. Mr. Caldwell and Mr. Roach want your ranch with its water rights, and when it became clear to them that your parents weren't going to sell, they decided to bring in Hawker and force the issue."

"Those rotten sonofabitches!" Monty hissed, struggling to sit up in the bed. "I got a gun and I'm going to get out of this bed, get dressed, and go kill them both!"

"Whoa up there!" Longarm said, raising both hands. "You can't do that."

"Why not! You just said that you think they're behind the murders of my parents."

"But I need proof before I can arrest them."

"They'll never tell you anything."

"Maybe and maybe not," Longarm argued. "I can be pretty persuasive when I have to be."

Monty studied him for a minute. "I'll bet you can. You'd probably beat the shit out of 'em like that red-haired giant beat the shit out of me."

"I'm a law officer. They have their rights. I'd have to be a little more subtle than a man like Hawker. But I have my ways."

"Sure you do," Monty said not bothering to hide his sarcasm. "Lawmen always have their ways."

Ignoring the caustic remark, Longarm said, "If I can

get to Cain Hawker before some bounty hunter puts a bullet in his gizzard, I might be able to make him talk."

"I'd sure like a crack at that big bastard," Monty said. "He murdered my parents and left me for dead. I got a sure enough score to settle with him, and I mean to do it without your help or that of anyone else."

But Longarm shook his head. "You're in rough shape, Monty. Just get healthy again and let me take care of Cain Hawker."

Monty Allison's jaw corded and he shook his head defiantly . "When I was almost dead, laying there choking in the blood and with both my eyes swollen shut, I swore that . . . if I lived . . . I'd find that man and kill him slow."

"Cain Hawker is going to take a lot of killing."

"Good! I want him to die in agony like he made my parents die," Monty said, his voice twisted with hatred. "I want to savor every moment remembering what he did to my ma and pa. And do you know something else, lawman?"

"No. Tell me," Longarm replied, troubled by the deep hatred and anger that Monty Allison was feeling inside, even though it was a well-justified hatred.

"Hawker *enjoyed* killing my folks. He was smiling when he did it to 'em, and he was smiling when he was beating me bloody. I've seen some tough men, Marshal Long. This is hard country with lots of real bad men, but that one is the toughest and the most evil person I've ever come across, and I'm going to be doing the world a favor when I take Cain Hawker's rotten life."

Longarm came to his feet and walked over to the door, which he'd left open a crack. He closed the door and went back to sit beside Monty. "The thing of it is, I'm an experienced lawman. I've done this sort of thing many times and I'm good at it. You, on the other hand, are not experienced and you'd be overmatched."

"That's what you think," Monty told him. "I heard that there's a two-hundred-dollar reward on Cain Hawker's head. Who better deserves killing him and collecting the reward than me? I could use the money to pay off the Bank of Yuma, save our Double A Ranch, and settle the score between us at the same time."

Longarm shook his head, anxious to talk the foolishness out of this kid. "If you even managed to find Cain Hawker, he or his Apache friends would kill you. Monty, you wouldn't stand a chance, and your sister will need you to help her save your family's ranch."

Monty considered that for a few long moments; then he slowly shook his bandaged head back and forth on his sweat-stained pillow. "Marshal Long, I know you're telling me to stay out of this because you don't want me killed, but—"

"Not only killed," Longarm interrupted, "but *tortured*. And make no mistake about it, they would torture you."

"I'm going after him just as soon as I can get on a horse," Monty said stubbornly. "I'm a good shot with rifle or pistol, and I've even practiced throwing a knife until I can put it in a tree at thirty feet nearly every throw."

"A tree?"

"Yeah," Monty said proudly. "An old half-breed has been teaching me how to throw a knife, and I've gotten damned good at it. Not as good as him, but damned good. The old half-breed says that I have a knack for it and I have real fast hands. I knew my hands were fast because I can shuck a six-gun about as fast as anyone in Yuma."

"I hear that you've got a whole set of cracked or busted ribs," Longarm observed. "So how do you throw a knife with any force or accuracy with busted ribs?"

Monty had a ready answer. "Cain Hawker busted me up only on the left side. I'm right-handed and throw with my right hand. I can still put a blade in his guts and stop him cold."

Longarm could see that there was no point in arguing with this kid. Monty Allison was filled with hatred and as stubborn as a Missouri mule. Never mind that he had no actual chance of finding or killing Cain Hawker. The kid would try, and then Cindy would have lost not only her parents, but also her kid brother.

"Look," Longarm said, reaching for his hat. "I'm tired from a long, long trip down from Colorado. Tomorrow morning, however, I'm going to try to find an old friend and ask him to hire me a tracker and hunter. I don't know this country all that well and I need a guide. Someone I can trust."

"You could trust me, and I do know this country pretty damn well," Monty insisted. "I could be your guide."

"No, that's not going to happen because you're too young, inexperienced, and you're badly hurt."

"Fine," Monty snapped. "If you don't want me along, then I'll be coming on my own."

"That would be a fatal mistake."

"I don't give a damn! Do you think I'm going to spend the rest of my life regretting that it wasn't me that settled the score on the man that murdered my folks?"

"I'm leaving," Longarm told the kid. "And you're staying. I'll send your sister back up here and tell her to talk some sense into that thick skull of yours."

"Are you screwing her?"

Longarm had been turning away when the question was thrown at him, and now he turned back. "What did you say, kid?"

"You heard me. Are you screwing my big sister?"

Their eyes locked in silent combat, and Longarm wanted to lie and tell the kid that he wasn't sleeping with Cindy, but he knew that the lie would be apparent, so he said, "She was shot on Colfax Avenue by Cain Hawker one morning as we were all going to work. I helped her out."

"You played the big white knight."

"I helped her out and took her to my rooms."

"Yeah, and your bed!" Monty said contemptuously. "What a hero and what a reward."

Longarm wanted to reach down and grab Monty Allison by the throat, but Hawker had already done that, so instead he just drew a deep breath and said, "Your sister is one of the bravest and finest women I've had the good fortune to meet in a long, long time. I helped her out. We have an . . . an attraction."

"You gonna marry my big sister and move onto the Double A?"

"No," Longarm said decisively. "When I've rounded up all the people responsible for your parents' death and your attack, then I'll make sure they either hang or go to that Yuma Prison for many years. After that is done, I'm returning to Denver, Colorado, and Pedro."

"Who's Pedro? Your Mexican manservant?"

"He's Cindy's tomcat and I've come to like him."

Monty rolled his eyes. "You're going to leave my sister and take up with her tomcat? What kind of a fool are you?"

Longarm shrugged his wide shoulders. "I like your sister very much. I want to make sure that she isn't hurt or killed and that you two don't lose your ranch."

"I bet you just want to keep screwing Cindy as long as you can," Monty said, turning his head away.

Longarm's fists knotted at his sides and he stood there in silent fury. "Monty, how come you're such a miserable shit? You've got a chip on your shoulder as big as a boulder, and I hear that it took a lot of money to keep you out of Yuma Prison."

Monty didn't answer, but Longarm could see the kid stiffen on his bed. Longarm wasn't finished. "If you don't get your head straight and start behaving like a man, then it won't matter that Cain Hawker didn't finish you off because someone else damn sure will."

"I don't need or want your advice!"

"You'd better take it, kid."

Monty turned around to glare at him. "You'd like me to think that you're some kind of hero or do-gooder. But you're not. You came out here because you like screwing my big sister. And I wouldn't be a damn bit surprised if you had your eye on our ranch!"

"I haven't even seen your damned ranch!" Longarm roared.

"Well, you know it's got some value, and I'll bet you don't own anything worth more than Pedro the cat."

"You're hopeless," Longarm said, turning on his heel.

"And you're a damned phony!" Monty yelled at Longarm as he was slamming out of the room. "You're not doing this out of the good of your heart! You've got your selfish motives just like everyone else in this rotten world!"

Longarm went down the stairs and faced Marshal Tom Beason, who was standing beside Cindy. They both saw the expression on Longarm's face and knew something was wrong.

"What happened?" Cindy asked.

"Nothing," Longarm said. "But the kid did tell me that the town's two most successful bankers are after the Double A. Apparently, they hold a note on your ranch worth nearly two hundred dollars."

"I could have told you that," Cindy said.

"Well," Longarm said, "I'm going to find a saloon and have a drink or two."

The pair looked at him with confusion. Finally, Tom Beason said, "Do you need some company?"

"No," Longarm snapped. "I don't. I'll see you both tomorrow morning at your office."

And with that, Longarm stomped out of the Rawhide Hotel and headed up the sunbaked and dusty street. He needed a drink . . . several drinks . . . and some time to think and cool down. Was there any truth in Monty's hateful accusation that the only reason he'd come to Yuma was to screw his big sister?

Hell, no! Well, at least not much truth in it anyway.

The bigger truth was that he really liked Cindy Allison and he hated to see anyone as nice as her being taken advantage of and almost killed.

Cain Hawker was a killer, and it was appearing more and more certain that a pair of scheming local bankers were out to get Cindy and Monty's Double A Ranch.

So those were good and noble reasons to have come to this blistering hellhole called Yuma. And by Gawd, he was going to see that justice was done in this place, and then he was returning to Denver and Pedro the cat.

It was just that right and just that simple, wasn't it? And if it was, then why in blazes had he let Monty Allison get under his skin so bad?

Longarm couldn't answer that question at the moment because he was mad as hell. He needed a few drinks and a few hours to reflect and simmer down. Then he'd work it all out, and tomorrow he would figure a way to go after Cain Hawker.

Chapter 12

It was late in the evening, and Longarm was sipping on the best brand of whiskey that could be bought in Yuma, when there was a knock at his door. Always cautious, he picked up his six-gun and tiptoed to the door in his bare feet. "Who is it?"

"It's me, Cindy. What's going on in there? You haven't found another woman already, have you?"

Longarm was in a grim mood, but the comment was enough to make him chuckle and he opened the door. "No, I haven't found another woman."

"Well, you sure acted surly when you came down from Monty's room, and I expected to see you for dinner, but you were nowhere to be found."

"Sorry," he said. "And I expect that Marshal Beason probably made up for my absence."

She cocked her head a little to one side and studied him. "Are you *jealous* of Tom?"

"Ha! I don't even know the meaning of the word. No, I'm not jealous. And as for my disappearing, I just needed some time off by myself to think about what I need to do."

"Do about what?"

"You and me and your embittered kid brother and Cain Hawker."

"What about you and me?"

Longarm shrugged. "Honestly, I didn't come to any conclusions. But your kid brother thinks that the only reason I came with you all the way from Colorado is because I want to keep screwing you, and maybe even get ownership of your ranch on the Gila River."

Cindy's eyes widened. "What?"

"You heard me. Monty thinks that I'm a no-good thief out to get what I can from you."

Cindy's cheeks colored with anger. "I'm going to speak to him the first thing tomorrow morning and give him a real piece of my mind. Monty has always been hotheaded and far too outspoken. I guess he hasn't changed since I left for Colorado."

"Well, there could be some truth in his accusations," Longarm said. "I mean, I really do like screwing you."

Her anger evaporated and she came into his arms and gave him a wet kiss. "The feeling is mutual. Are you still sober enough to do it?"

"Do hogs love mud? Sure I am!"

"Then let's not let the whole evening go to waste."

Moments later, they were both in Longarm's hotel bed having a wonderful romp. Longarm was tired, and so was Cindy, from their long, hard journey, but as their passions mounted, their fatigue melted away, and before they were finished, Longarm and Cindy were both whooping in wild and sweaty ecstasy. Quivering and emptying the last of his seed into her warm, strong body, Longarm rolled over with a groan of satisfaction while the Arizona ranch girl stretched like a tawny lioness.

"Yeah," she said a little later, "it works for us just as well in Yuma as well as it ever did in Denver."

"I'm not surprised. Are you?"

"No," she said. "Not really. But I thought we both decided that, when this nightmare was all over, you would return to your job in Denver and I'd stay here on my family ranch."

"Yeah, that was decided." He rolled over on his side and studied her pretty face. "Or at least, I thought it was. Have you had second thoughts about staying in Yuma?"

"Not really. This is where I belong, and I don't suppose you've had second thoughts about leaving Denver for Arizona."

"I'm sorry," he told her. "But I can't take this heat and dry country. Tom Beason might find it healthful, but it sucks the energy right out of me, and I much prefer the high mountains and crisp air of Denver."

They were silent for a while, and then Longarm said, "The reason I was really troubled when I came down from the lobby wasn't just what your brother accused me of."

"Then what was it?"

"Your brother is filled with anger and hatred for anyone who carries a badge or has some authority."

"I know. He's been that way since he was very young."

"Any reason why?"

"Our father was a hard and uncompromising man,"

Cindy told him. "He ordered Mother and us kids around like we were slaves. And we always had to say 'yes, sir' to him. He was a good man, but unyielding and often quick-tempered and violent. He would backhand you if you disobeyed, or maybe get his razor strop and beat the hell out of your ass."

"He did that to you?"

"Plenty of times. But I always got off easy compared to how he disciplined poor Monty. Many was the time when he whipped Monty so hard that Mother and I jumped in between them and had to stop him. My father would go crazy at times, and as we began to get into financial trouble, he got more and more short-tempered and unreasonable. He took his anger out on all of us, but Monty suffered the worst for it."

"That explains his hatred of authority then," Longarm said. "He's real hard inside, Cindy. He asks no quarter nor does he want any quarter. And the worst part of it is that he has sworn to hunt down and kill Cain Hawker."

"Monty wouldn't stand a chance against that man."

"That's what I tried to explain to your brother, but he wouldn't listen. He says he's going after Hawker the minute he can stand up and leave town."

"I'll talk to him."

"It won't help," Longarm told her. "He's very determined and stubborn. And he talked about being fast with a six-gun and a knife."

"He is," Cindy said. "My father believed in an eye for an eye and he knew how to use a gun or rifle. The only thing that he and Monty had in common was their love of weapons and the use of them in fighting. My father wouldn't give Monty the time of day and worked him like a slave . . . but he always bought Monty ammunition to practice with, and made sure he had the best pistol and rifle he could find. Monty is very good with weapons. I've often watched him draw and shoot his pistol in the blink of an eye."

Longarm said, "Your brother also bragged that he was very good at throwing a knife."

"That's true. A half-breed Apache spent hours and hours teaching him how to use a knife to either fight or throw. Monty loves his knives, especially the throwing knives. He and the half-breed even used my father's forge and anvil to fashion knives, some of which are pretty scary-looking weapons."

Longarm considered all this and came to a swift conclusion. "I guess it's good that Monty is fast with a gun or knife," Longarm said. "But it didn't help him save himself or your parents at the ranch house when Cain Hawker arrived and left them all for dead."

"No, it didn't. But whatever else you might think of Monty, he's smart and he would never make the same mistake twice."

"I can't have him to worry about on top of Hawker," Longarm said. "I tried to talk some sense into your brother and failed. Now, it's up to you."

"Monty has never listened to me, and I see no reason why he would now."

Longarm shrugged. "Then we'll let the cards fall where they may. I just won't take responsibility for him."

"I understand. Can I sleep with you tonight?"

"Sure thing."

"I've kinda gotten to like it, you know."

"I know," Longarm replied. "Because I have, too."

"Maybe you should rethink your position on not wanting to leave Denver."

"Or you should rethink yours and come back to Denver," Longarm replied.

They both smiled and prepared for sleep.

"Custis?"

"Yeah."

"How are you going to take up Cain Hawker's trail tomorrow?"

"I'm not sure," he said honestly. "But a giant with red hair is not someone that goes around without catching a lot of attention. I'll do what I often do starting out, and that's going around to the saloons and whorehouses and asking about Hawker."

"And people there would actually tell you the truth?"

"Sure. At the saloons I buy a beer or two and tip the bartender handsomely."

"And what do you do at the whorehouses?" Cindy asked, eyeing him closely.

"I buy 'em a drink and pay 'em a compliment and maybe a few dollars if they have anything I want."

"You're speaking of *information*. Right?"

"That's right," Longarm said, laughing.

"Just as long as we have that straight," Cindy told him. "Because if you're going to go around poking Yuma's whores, I don't want anything more to do with you."

"I understand and I never pay a whore for her services and I'm not about to start tomorrow."

"Glad to hear it," Cindy told him as she snuggled up

close. "You know I'm going to worry myself sick about you when you're gone."

"Don't do that," he said. "I'm perfectly capable of doing my job and coming back to you in one piece."

"That's all I wanted to hear," she said. "Now, we'd better get some sleep."

"I agree. Just keep a close eye on your kid brother. I don't want him messing things up for me."

"I will. Besides, the doctor says that he's in no condition to go anywhere for at least a month."

"It'll take me a lot less time than that to arrest or kill Cain Hawker."

Cindy yawned. "I sure do hope so. I surely do."

Longarm fell into a dreamless sleep. The manhunt would start first thing tomorrow morning.

Chapter 13

Longarm spent the next morning walking up and down the streets of Yuma talking to shopkeepers and merchants about Cain Hawker. The local gunsmith, an older man named Dawson with prominent beetlelike brows and a small goatee, readily admitted that he knew Cain Hawker well.

"Sure, Cain visits my shop plenty often. The man keeps his weapons in good condition, and is always looking to upgrade them with whatever is newest and best. Hawker is a scary fella, but we have always gotten along fine because he loves to talk about guns and pistols and he does have money to spend. For that reason alone, I always treated him as one of my best customers."

Longarm leaned on the glass counter and studied the assortment of used and new pistols with interest. "You know that I'm a deputy United States marshal, don't you?"

"Sure. Word gets around fast in Yuma. Everybody wants to know everything about everyone. There are damn few secrets in this town. Marshal, instead of beating around the bush, why don't you just come out and ask me what you want to know?"

"All right," Longarm agreed. "For starters, what kind of pistol does Hawker carry?"

"He packs a Colt revolver, same caliber as the one you're packin' on your left hip."

"Does Hawker carry hideout guns?"

The gunsmith studied Longarm for a minute before answering. "Marshal, I guess you're going after him and want to know exactly what you're up against, huh?"

"That's right. He's the one that killed Mr. and Mrs. Allison out at the Double A Ranch and almost beat Monty Allison to death."

"Yeah, that's the word I got, too," the gunsmith said. "I liked them both, but I can't say the same about Monty."

"Do you know the kid well?"

"As well as anyone, I expect, which really isn't very well at all. What you need to understand is that Monty Allison fancies himself as a shootist. He comes in here all the time wanting me to rework the pull pressure on his trigger. He had me adjust the spring so his gun would fire with almost no pressure. I told him it was dangerous, but he wanted it done all the same. I filed the front sight off his barrel, and I made him a special holster that broke away in the front so that he could draw and fire his gun even faster."

"His sister says that he is not only fast, but accurate."

"Oh, yeah. I've gone out with Monty twice to watch him shoot, and he's as good as I've ever seen."

"Is Cain Hawker fast with his pistol?"

"Naw." The gunsmith shook his head. "Cain is so big that he's slow. But I'm sure he's accurate. And you were asking about a hideout gun. Well, Cain does carry a derringer in his boot and another up his left sleeve."

"Double-barreled derringers?"

"That's right. And he favors a double-barreled shotgun."

"Does he hang out with anyone special around here?"

Dawson shook his head. "Cain is far too mean and violent for anyone to want to hang around him. Even the Apache can barely tolerate the man, and the ones he rides with are the worst kind of savages."

"I'm going after Hawker," Longarm said. "In your opinion, should I start by crossing the border and taking up the hunt in Old Mexico?"

"That's what I'd do if I were you," Dawson said. "Hawker came in here pretty drunk one time and he started bragging about how he had a señorita and some good ranch land about twenty miles south of the border near a little village called Mirador. He says that he is the richest man in that village and he has many friends there and treats them well. He bragged that he even supports the Catholic church and donated money for their small adobe chapel. But to tell you the truth, my impression of Cain Hawker is that he is the spawn of Satan."

"Yeah," Longarm agreed. "But by donating to the local village church, he's being smart and gaining the loyalty of the people of Mirador. He knows that, if the Mexican Army comes looking to arrest him, the priest and the parishioners will stand up in his defense."

"I suppose that's true," Dawson said. "Hawker also claims that the renegade Apache know not to raid Mirador or steal from its poor farming people."

"Is Hawker most often in the company of Apache?"

Dawson shrugged. "That's hard to say. I've seen him alone often enough. But most likely, you'll see him with an Apache or two. They're a tough looking bunch, but they can't be arrested just because they're Indians. I've heard that most of them are ex-U.S. Army scouts, and so they're hated by their own Apache people who live on the reservations."

Longarm nodded with understanding. "Did you know that there is a two-hundred-dollar reward on Cain Hawker's head?"

"Yeah. And I'm sure that's why I haven't seen him around in a few weeks. And there's something else you should know. I've had at least three bounty hunters in here getting their weapons in fighting shape and swearing they are going to find Hawker and collect that big reward."

"Yeah," Longarm said, "I expect I'll cross trails with a few of them before this is all over."

"They're a bad bunch, those bounty hunters. Almost as bad as Hawker himself."

"I know."

Longarm turned for the door, then paused and looked back at the gunsmith. "Dawson?"

"Yeah?"

"Anything else you care to tell me about Hawker?"

"Only that I don't expect to ever see you walking through that door again. If Cain doesn't kill you, the Apache he runs with sure as hell will. And if by some chance you should avoid them, then the Mexicans will kill you for certain because they hate all badge-totin' gringos."

"Thanks for the encouraging words," Longarm said cryptically.

"You're welcome. And if I was you, my next stop would be at Bert Mason's funeral parlor. Pay him in advance and tell him what you want carved on your tombstone."

Longarm almost laughed. "You'd probably say I should have him carve HERE LIES A FOOL on my tombstone."

Dawson shrugged with indifference, and picked up a gun that someone had dropped off for repairs. "Marshal, I regret to say that wouldn't be too far off the mark."

"Well," Longarm said, opening the door, "Hawker almost killed Cindy Allison in Denver and her brother at the ranch. And he *did* kill the parents. Have you ever seen Hawker coming or going at the Bank of Yuma?"

"As a matter of fact, I have," Dawson said. "Like most of us, he has an account there and makes his deposits. I wouldn't doubt that he has a bigger bank balance than either one of us, but I'm sure that the bank's manager, Mr. Caldwell, won't divulge that information even to a United States marshal."

"If Hawker does have a large bank balance in his account," Longarm said, "then it's blood money."

"Maybe so, Marshal, but it'll spend just as well as an honest workingman's wages."

When Longarm went outside, the sun was well up in the eastern sky and the temperature was already nudging one hundred. He removed his Stetson and wiped sweat from his brow, and then decided he might as well go pay Mr. Caldwell and Mr. Roach a visit at the bank. It was just down the street, and was built of adobe and stone like many of the town's other permanent buildings.

"Good morning," Longarm said, smiling at the teller when he approached the counter. "I'd like to have a word with your bank's manager, Mr. Caldwell."

The teller eyed him closely. "And you would be?"

Longarm showed the man his badge. "Deputy United States Marshal Custis Long."

"I'll see if Mr. Caldwell is available."

"Tell him to make sure that he's 'available,'" Longarm said, dropping the smile.

"Yes, sir."

Longarm had to cool his heels for ten minutes while he waited to see Mr. Caldwell. Then he was escorted into a fine private office and left to sit another ten minutes waiting.

"Marshal," a handsome man in his late forties said, rushing into the office and extending his hand. "Sorry to have kept you waiting but I was in the middle of an accounting session that required my undivided attention this morning. What can I do to help you?"

Longarm decided to get right to the point. "I would like to know anything you can tell me about one of your depositors . . . Mr. Cain Hawker."

The banker momentarily froze, then quickly recovered and sat down behind his large desk. "Yes, he's being sought for the murders of Mr. and Mrs. Allison."

"That's right, and I'm sure you know that there is a large reward on his head."

"I know that, but what I meant was, why are you asking me about the man instead of tracking him down?"

"I have a feeling that he wasn't the only one involved in the Allison ranch murders."

"What are you talking about?"

"I think he murdered them for someone else," Longarm replied. "I believe that Cain Hawker was a hired assassin."

"Care for a cigar, Marshal?"

"As a matter of fact I do," Longarm said, noting how Caldwell's hand suddenly had a slight tremor as he removed a pair of cigars from his humidor and passed one across his desk.

"Marshal, these are from Kentucky."

Longarm inhaled the cigar's aroma and nodded with approval. "Fine tobacco," he said as he slipped the cigar into his vest pocket. "I'll enjoy it tonight after dinner."

"Good. I recommend the Desert Steak House. The food is excellent, which can't be said for most of the places to eat here in Yuma."

"Appreciate the tip and the smoke," Longarm said. "Now, where were we in this conversation?"

"You said something about maybe someone hiring Cain Hawker to murder the poor Allison couple. To be honest, I have no idea why you would think such a thing."

"Well," Longarm began, "Cain isn't a house burglar. According to Marshal Tom Beason, there was nothing of value taken from the Double A, so the motive for murder wasn't theft."

"Hawker is known to have quite a temper and has a record of violence," the banker mused. "He probably went to the Double A seeking a favor of some kind and when it was refused, he flew into a rage and . . . well, things got out of hand and resulted in a terrible and tragic double murder. Thank heavens that the boy looks as if he will pull through and make a complete recovery."

Longarm's chin dipped in agreement. "Do you have any other ideas why Hawker might go to the Double A and kill that old couple?"

"Of course not."

Caldwell nipped off the end of his cigar and studied it thoughtfully before continuing. "When I first learned of the crime, I simply concluded that Hawker and Mr. Allison . . . who, by the way, had a very bad temper himself despite his advanced age . . . became embroiled in some argument that turned into a full blown confrontation."

"If that was the case," Longarm asked, "why would Hawker murder Mrs. Allison and leave her son for dead?"

Caldwell lit his cigar, fingers betraying a slight tremor. "I have no idea. Perhaps Monty Allison interfered in the argument and Hawker just went blood-crazy."

"That could be the cause of it all," Longarm replied, not believing it for a minute. "But I think that Cain Hawker was *sent* to the Double A to wipe out the entire family so that the ranch would have to go on the auction block."

"What an interesting theory," Caldwell said, blowing a cloud of blue smoke at his ceiling. "Any proof to back that wild theory up?"

"Not yet. However, I understand that your bank holds a sizable note on the Double A Ranch, and in fact you and a Mr. Roach have actually tried to purchase the ranch."

"Ha! My assistant and I are bankers! Why on earth would we want the Double A Ranch? Really, Marshal, your imagination is running amok here."

"Is it?" Longarm asked, his tone losing its friendliness. "Miss Allison tells me that her ranch has the best water rights on the Gila and that when they ran cattle, the Double A was quite a profitable ranch."

"That may be so, but it's really none of my concern and, to be honest, I don't see that it should be your concern either."

Longarm didn't appreciate being told what or what not was his concern. "Mr. Caldwell, as the holder of a large note on the Double A, I should think that the profitability and value of those water rights would be very important to the Bank of Yuma. If the property and its water rights weren't quite valuable, why would you make a sizable loan on the property?"

Caldwell smiled with patient tolerance. "Because that's what a bank does . . . make loans and service the people of its community. This bank doesn't exist to decorate Yuma. We are here to help build this community, and that involves making loans on real estate."

"I'm sure that's true," Longarm agreed. "But according to my sources, you and your assistant were aggressively trying to buy the Double A. However, Mr. Allison wasn't in the least bit interested in selling."

Caldwell tapped the ash from his cigar into a fine ashtray and then said, "Mr. Allison had many fine quali-

ties, but being a smart businessman was not one of
them. He was going to lose his ranch, Marshal. I, as the
bank's manager, was trying to help Mr. Allison recoup
something for himself and his aged wife, both of whom
were in failing health. We . . . myself and Mr. Roach . . .
were concerned about the old couple, and were trying to
buy their ranch and pay off the note so that they were
not foreclosed upon and left penniless."

"How noble of you and Mr. Roach," Longarm said,
barely managing to keep the sarcasm out of his voice.

"Yes, well, they were nice people, and I knew that
our bank had no choice but to foreclose, in which case
they would have received almost nothing for all their
years of hard work. We offered Mr. Allison a very good
price for the Double A Ranch, and now that he and his
wife are deceased, I hope that Miss Allison will bring all
of this to a close and sell, because our generous offer
still stands. But it won't stand much longer."

"Oh?"

"That's right," Caldwell said. "As a matter of fact, I
was going to see Miss Allison today and tell her that our
offer is only good until the end of this month. She is the
sole inheritor of the Double A, and it is her decision to
sell or not sell the ranch."

Longarm leaned forward with genuine interest. "Are
you saying that Monty Allison was left completely out
of his parents' will?"

Caldwell frowned. "When the young man got into
serious trouble and his parents had to spend so much
money keeping him out of the Yuma Prison, then he
was dropped from the will, except for some small personal belongings and a few horses he would inherit."

"I see. And my guess is that you are quite familiar with the will."

"I am because I needed to be," Caldwell said bluntly. "A copy of the will is deposited in our bank's vault."

"I'd like to see it."

"I'm afraid that is not possible without a court order, and the judge is currently out of town."

Longarm came to his feet and stared down at the banker. "I won't leave until this case is solved."

"What's to solve?" Caldwell demanded. "It's obvious that Cain Hawker murdered the old couple. Find and kill the man."

"I'd rather take him *alive*," Longarm said. "Not only because it is my job to arrest and bring criminals to trial, but also because I want to hear from Cain's own lips why he killed the Allison couple that day and if he was acting alone."

Caldwell forced a weak smile. "Do you have any idea of where to find him?"

Longarm thought of the small village called Mirador, but he shook his head. "Afraid not yet."

"Well, this is a big, hot, and dangerous country down here, so good luck, Marshal."

"Luck doesn't have a hell of a lot to do with hunting down a killer," Longarm replied. "I'll see you again, Mr. Caldwell. Thank you for your time."

"My pleasure."

Moments later, Longarm walked out of the bank manager's office even more convinced than ever that Caldwell and his assistant were the ones who had hired the giant redheaded assassin.

Chapter 14

That afternoon, the temperature soared to well over 115 degrees in the shade, and Longarm would have liked nothing better than to take refuge in a saloon and nurse a cold beer. But he had a job to finish, so he bought supplies and then a good saddle horse and little pack burro from a man who looked to be in his late thirties and who was still handsome in a world-weary sort of way.

"Marshal, I heard that you're going after Cain Hawker," the liveryman said when Longarm was ready to ride out of Yuma.

"That's right."

"Which direction are you headed?"

"South into Mexico."

The man eyed Longarm's new Winchester repeating rifle and the ammunition belt slung around his shoulder. "You're riding straight into a hornet's nest."

Longarm shrugged. "If that's where I'm going to find Cain Hawker, then I don't see that I have any choice in the matter."

"Sure you do," the liveryman drawled, spitting a

brown stream of tobacco into a pile of horse shit. "If you were smart, you'd hunker down here in Yuma and stay out of the heat. Sooner or later, Cain Hawker will come riding back across the border, and then you might even have a fair chance at killin' the big bastard."

"Well," Longarm said, "I don't fancy the idea of sitting around this hellhole for long, hot months waiting for Hawker to appear. I'm the kind of man that likes to take action, not wait for it."

The liveryman chewed his plug thoughtfully, then finally said, "I hear tell that Cain Hawker owns some land and cattle in Mirador and that he takes care of the people in that village in exchange for them watching out for him. That means that you won't have anybody to help you south of the border. If I was a few years younger and didn't have this damn stable to work me into the ground, then I might even tag along with you for half that two-hundred-dollar reward. I am a fair-to-middling shot with a pistol and pretty damned good with a rifle."

"Is that a fact?"

"It is," the liveryman said. "But I'm not a professional like you, and I'm not even close to being in Monty Allison's category as a shootist."

Longarm nodded with understanding. "I'm sure you are brave and a good shot, but I like working alone. And I'll tell you something else, seeing as how you've told me a thing or two. Given Cain Hawker's vicious and murderous nature, I can't believe that he hasn't made some bad enemies in Mirador."

"That's probably true enough," the liveryman agreed. He extended his hand up to Longarm. "I hope you find and kill that big sonofabitch. He's the Devil himself and should have been shot long ago. If you are the one to do 'er, then most everyone will say 'good riddance' and you're plenty entitled to that two-hundred-dollar reward."

"Thanks."

"Just follow the Colorado River about twenty miles and you'll come to the small town of San Luis. Watch out there for thieves and wicked women. There are a few honest men and women in San Luis, but not many, and the bad ones love to see a lone gringo passing through. They regard 'em like turkey on the table. They'll promise you wild women and tequila, but you'd be smart to turn both offers down and keep riding until you come to a purple mountain range. Bear to the east and you'll see the small town of Mirador about five miles away. Does Cain Hawker know you on sight?"

Longarm considered the question. "I'm not sure. We had a run-in that lasted just a moment or two in Denver when he tried to kill Miss Allison. But it all happened so fast that I'm not sure he would recognize me clear down in Mexico."

"If he doesn't, it will be a big advantage. My advice is just to draw your gun and shoot Cain down the instant you lay eyes on the man and then ride like hell for the border. It's your only chance."

"I'm a federal lawman, not a bounty hunter. What I plan to do is arrest the man and then bring him back to hang. How likely is it that he'll have some of his Apache friends close by?"

"Damned likely," the liveryman said. "And they're mean ones that would rather torture a man to death slow than kill him fast."

"I expect that is true."

Longarm wrapped the lead rope to his pack burro around his saddle horn and started to leave, but the liveryman said, "Hold up a second. There's one more thing I want to tell you, Marshal."

"That being?"

"There is a woman named Juanita Lopez who owns the biggest cantina in Mirador. I knew her real well at one time and I helped her buy that cantina. If you tell her you're my friend, she might help you out if you get caught up in big trouble. Tell her that Barney Holt is going to come down and see her one of these days when the weather cools and the soft rains begin to fall. Tell her that I'm doing fine up here in Yuma, and still have some lead in my pencil that I'm holding especially for her."

Holt blushed a little and added, "Juanita will know what I mean."

Longarm laughed. "I'll sure do that."

"You can trust Juanita. She's not one to forget that I helped her when she was just a common whore headed for an early and unmarked grave. Fact is, we saved each other from a bad end."

"Are you really going to go down and visit her when the weather improves?"

"Hell," the liveryman said, hitching up his britches and spitting into the pile again. "I've been thinking of selling this business and going down there to marry Juanita. I'm pretty sure I'm going to go ahead and do 'er this fall. My livery sure isn't making me rich, and truth be told, I don't even like horses, much less shoveling horse shit twice a day."

Longarm studied the run-down livery and saw nothing but hard times and way too much work. "Then selling out and moving down into Mexico might be the right thing to do."

"Juanita and I are still young enough to have a few kids. I'd have married the woman a long time ago if it hadn't been for Cain Hawker living down there. He and I would start shooting at each other. My problem is that Cain is a better man with a gun than I am."

"Maybe so, but he makes a hell of a big target."

Holt smiled at that remark and said, "So do you, Marshal. So do you."

After saying good-bye to Cindy Allison, Longarm rode out of Yuma in the blistering heat of the late afternoon. By following the river, he knew he could always have water, and several times before dark he rode into the Colorado just to cool off. Darkness fell, and Longarm rode along a moonlit and well-traveled road until he finally came to a stone marker that had a little sign announcing the border with Mexico.

He kept riding until he saw the lights of San Luis just up ahead. He circled the town and pushed on for Mirador. Finally, just around midnight, he saw that town's lights. He could hear music and laughter, and knew that it had to be coming from one of the cantinas. Longarm was weary and his face was creased with salty sweat. What he really needed was a good night's sleep and a fine meal of tortillas and beans all washed down with tequila . . . but not too much of it, because he was a gringo and had to be constantly alert and on his guard. Even before Barney Holt's warning, Longarm knew that

he was entering a dangerous land where many a gringo
had just been robbed, murdered, and left to rot in the hot
sun. Life wasn't worth a whole hell of a lot along the
Mexican border, and Longarm meant to ride back across
it all in one piece.

Because of the lateness of the hour, he attracted little
attention as he entered Mirador. An old man came up to
him, and Longarm knew just enough Spanish to employ
the old fellow to watch over his horses and supplies and
tell him where he could find Señorita Lopez.

The old man was bent and very thin. He had silver
hair and wore a serape around his narrow shoulders.
When Longarm gave him money for his information
and help, the peasant grinned, revealing that he was almost toothless.

"Gracias, señor! Gracias!"

Longarm carried his rifle into the cantina, which was
the largest in town. He was not the only American in
the cantina, and for that he was somewhat grateful.
There were men and women of all ages and descrip-
tions, most of them young and loud with the liquor
firing their bravado.

"Beer," he said to the bartender, pointing to the
man's glass next to him.

"Sí, señor."

When the beer arrived, Longarm paid for it in
American coin, and made sure that he gave the bartender a generous tip.

"Tequila?" the attentive bartender asked several
times.

But Longarm shook his head, then said, "Señorita
Lopez?"

The bartender pointed to a handsome Mexican woman in her mid-thirties with shiny black hair, which was pulled back from her forehead with a pearl comb.

Longarm went over to introduce himself. "Our friend Barney Holt said to say hello and that he was coming down to see you."

Juanita Lopez smiled broadly, and did not try to hide the excitement in her voice. "Barney is coming? How soon!"

Her English was so perfect that Longarm thought he might as well have been speaking to a woman on the streets of Denver. "Barney said he was selling his livery stable this fall and coming down to Mirador show to you he still had plenty of lead in his pencil."

Juanita burst into hilarious laughter. Laughter so unrestrained and loud that it caused many in her smoky and noisy cantina to turn and stare with curiosity.

She winked at Longarm, and poked him in the ribs almost playfully. "Barney is a good man and an even better lover."

Longarm didn't know what to say about that, so he just nodded and sipped his beer.

"You're really his friend?"

"I bought a horse, burro, and outfit from him," Longarm explained. "We seemed to hit it off pretty good and he said he sure was missing you."

"I miss him, too! Many times I think maybe I sell this cantina and go up to Yuma to see my Barney. But I don't like that place much, and maybe that is not a good idea."

"I'd wait for him to come to you," Longarm advised. "Is there a good place to eat and to sleep in Mirador that you can recommend?"

"I have rooms to rent," she told him. "But if you are a friend of Barney's, then you are also my friend and you stay for free. You look hot and tired. Come with me, please."

"I have my horse and burro along with supplies outside. I'd better not just leave them, or they will be gone by morning."

"I will make sure that they are safe." Juanita motioned for a man wearing a huge sombrero to come over, and then in rapid Spanish she told him to take care of Longarm's animals and belongings.

"Come with me," she said, turning back to Longarm. "What is your name?"

"Custis Long."

"Custis is a nice name. I will show you to a clean room and if you like, I will have food sent up to you. And how about a clean and pretty young señorita?"

"Sounds good, but I'll pass on the señorita. The hour is very late and I wouldn't do myself-proud."

She raised an eyebrow and said, "Maybe tomorrow morning I will send her to your room and see if you are feeling rested enough to 'do yourself proud.'"

Longarm grinned sheepishly. "Actually, I'm going to be taking care of some important business tomorrow morning."

"Business? What kind of business?"

She was eyeing him closely, and Longarm made a quick decision to put his complete trust this woman. He leaned in toward her ear and whispered, "I'm here to arrest Cain Hawker. Can you tell me where to find him?"

Her eyes widened with either fear or surprise, and

she took his arm and hurried him out of her cantina. "You are a *lawman*?"

"Yes, I am."

She whispered, "Do not tell anyone!"

"All right. But I'm still going to arrest Hawker or die trying tomorrow morning."

"You will die trying," Juanita said in a low and grave voice. "Maybe you should not do such a foolish thing here in Mirador where Cain has many friends."

"You being one of them?"

"No!" she said in a fierce and hushed whisper. "I hate that man. If it were not for him, my Barney would be here right now. But if he came, Cain would shoot him down like a street dog."

"That's pretty much what Barney said."

Juanita led him around behind the cantina to a small hotel. "I also own and live in this place," she explained. "If you are a lawman, you are not safe in Mexico, and especially here in Mirador."

"That's what everyone keeps telling me."

"Because it is true! You are either very handsome or very stupid. Come with me and talk to no one else tonight."

Longarm allowed himself to be led into the little hotel, and then past a man dozing in a corner and into a room that was very colorful and filled with scented candles. "This is a room you rent out?"

"No! It is *my* room, Custis! You would not be safe anywhere else tonight. Stay here and food will come soon."

"Okay."

She took both of his big hands in her own. "Why

didn't Barney try to stop you from coming down here? It is madness!"

"He didn't try because he knew that it would be a waste of his time," Longarm answered. "I've come all the way from Colorado to either arrest or kill Hawker, and I'm not turning back until one or the other is done."

Juanita Lopez shook her head in bafflement. "You are too handsome to die so young."

"I'm not the one about to die," Longarm assured her. "Tomorrow could well be Cain Hawker's last day."

"Such brave talk!" she scolded. "Don't you know that he has friends who protect him?"

"Apache renegades, I'm told."

"Yes! Very bad men!"

"I'll deal with 'em if I have to," Longarm vowed. "I've dealt with bad Indians before and come out standing up."

She looked up at him with eyes reflecting pity. "You should have a woman tonight, for she would be your last taste."

Longarm just smiled. "Are you coming back to this room tonight?"

"No."

"Too bad," he told her in a manner that left no doubt he was teasing. "If I thought you were going to be my last woman, I'd be sorely tempted to wait up for you."

Juanita giggled and kissed his cheek. "You are a handsome man with a silver tongue. No?"

"Just being honest," he said.

"Food will be here soon," she promised. "You must eat and sleep late. Tomorrow, you will need to be quick and strong. Very quick and strong."

"I thank you for your help," he said. "And I can see why Barney wants to come down here and marry you."

"Marry?"

"Yes. That's what he told me."

Juanita's dark eyes lit up with joy. "I will marry him! We talked of children and a different life we could have together farther down in Mexico, where the air is cooler, everything is green, and the rains fall almost every afternoon."

"It will happen," Longarm said.

She was so excited by this news that she kissed Longarm once more, this time on the lips. He almost wrapped her up in his arms and tried to push the matter a little further, but his good breeding and good sense warned him that two kisses and tonight's protection were as much as he should expect from Juanita Lopez.

Chapter 15

Yuma Marshal Tom Beason stood back and listened to a heated argument between Miss Cindy Allison and her troubled kid brother, Monty. The kid wanted to crawl out of his bed, get dressed, and then light out for Mirador so that he could have the glory of gunning down Cain Hawker. Never mind that Monty wasn't nearly fit enough to ride that far, much less kill the assassin of his parents. The kid was angry and stubborn. Cindy, on the other hand, was adamant that her younger brother remain bedridden here in Yuma and let the cards fall where they may down in Mexico.

"Monty, I know that you feel that you need to get even with Hawker," Cindy was saying. "But you can't possibly hate him any more than I do, and I won't have you throwing your life away out of revenge."

"But it isn't right that Marshal Long went down there all alone!" Monty shouted. "This is as much our fight as it is his."

Cindy shook her head in sharp disagreement. "Custis has the experience and the ability to find and either arrest or kill Cain Hawker. That's what he does for a living. He's good at it, and I believe that he will be successful and return to us alive in the next few days."

"But I don't believe that!" Monty raged. "I'm sure that Marshal Long is not as fast or accurate with a gun as I am. *I* should be the one going down there to kill that giant sonofabitch for murdering our parents."

"You're all the family I have left," Cindy told him, eyes wet with tears as she tried to take and hold her brother's hand. "Custis told me that he preferred to work alone. He promised me that he would either return with Hawker or kill him down in Mexico."

Monty pulled his hand roughly away from that of his sister. "But what if your hero Marshal Long fails? What if he's already been captured and needs our help? We both know that Hawker has Apache friends. You can't expect one man to go down there and come back across the border alive."

"Monty, that's *exactly* what I expect. Let's give Custis a chance!"

"But that's what I'm trying to tell you!" Monty yelled. "One man against Hawker and those Apache friends of his doesn't stand even the slightest chance. I need to go help him."

"No," Cindy said, clenching her fists and then slamming them down on the bed. "Custis wanted to do this alone, and you are not in any shape to ride, much less face a pack of killers."

Monty looked past his sister to Beason with a mixture of anger and pleading radiating in his eyes. "Marshal Beason, you should have gone down there after Cain Hawker! You should have insisted that you go along with Marshal Long to arrest or kill that murdering sonofabitch."

"I'm hired by the people of Yuma to protect them and their property," Beason explained once more. "Believe me, I really wanted to go with Custis, but my job doesn't allow it."

"Then quit your damned job and go anyway!" Monty cried. "Don't you understand that no matter how good or experienced a lawman Custis Long might be, he has no chance whatsoever down there in Mexico?"

Beason ground his teeth. "I'm sorry, Monty. I just can't leave Yuma unprotected."

"You won't even be missed for a few days. We could go down there, help Marshal Long out, and bring back Cain Hawker draped across a saddle. He *murdered* my folks! You need to help bring him to justice . . . or are you just too afraid of Hawker and that's the real reason you won't leave Yuma?"

Tom Beason's cheeks flushed with anger. "I'm not afraid. I'm just trying to do the job that I was sworn to do and that job is to protect—"

"Stop that bullshit!" Monty barked, cutting the local marshal off. "You're afraid of going into Mexico after Hawker. That's the real reason why you aren't riding with Custis Long. Admit it!"

Beason threw up his hands in exasperation. "Cindy," he said, "your brother isn't making any sense. He's angry and running off at the mouth. I'm going back to my office. If you need me for anything at all, stop by and wake me up. Otherwise, I'll see you at breakfast tomorrow."

"All right, Tom." She walked him to the door and out

into the narrow upstairs hallway, whispering, "Please don't be too hard on my brother, Tom. Look at what was done to him and my parents. Is there any wonder that Monty is upset and set on vengeance at any cost?"

"I suppose not," Tom said quietly. "But it's still damned hard to stand there and be labeled a coward."

"Yes, I know you're not a coward and the reason you didn't want to ride with Custis is because of your sworn responsibilities. But . . ."

Her voice trained away.

"But *what,* Cindy? Do you think I made the wrong decision not to ride with Marshal Long down to Mirador?"

"I don't know what the right decision for you was. I just know that I am terribly afraid that Custis hasn't got a chance down there alone."

Tom groaned with frustration. He had become very attracted and attached to Cindy Allison, and now she was letting him know that she thought he might have made a mistake by staying in Yuma. A mistake caused by his responsibilities as Yuma's marshal? Or by his real fear of going into Mexico after Hawker and dying?

Cindy placed her hand on Tom's forearm. "I'm sure you did what you thought was right, Tom. That's all any of us can do."

"Sure," he replied, shaking his head and walking off down the hallway, feeling a sense of undeniable shame. "Sure I did."

Three hours later, Monty Allison took a few deep breaths and stood up fully dressed in his second-floor hotel room. He felt a bit light-headed, but the pain in his head was gone, leaving only a dull throbbing in his side from the broken but rapidly mending ribs. Pulling on his boots had been the worst part, but he'd managed to do it, and now he moved to his window and gazed down into Yuma's main street. It was after midnight, and there wasn't a single soul moving on the sidewalks, and the moon was full and cast a weak yellow glow on the buildings. Yuma, he thought, at its finest hour.

It's time to get down to Mirador and settle the score with Cain Hawker.

Monty had given up trying to reason with either his sister or Marshal Beason earlier that evening. He'd attempted over and over to tell them that he simply could not lie in a bed and let Marshal Custis Long face Cain Hawker and his Apache friends alone down in Mexico.

So now, as Monty strapped on his custom-made gun belt and spun the well-oiled cylinder of his Colt revolver, he knew that he was going to take matters into his own hands. By now, Custis Long might already be dead in Mirador, or even worse, lashed to a torture rack while the Apache had their wicked way flaying and skinning his body. There simply was no more time to waste, and Monty had a mission rather than just a plan.

Unsure if he could ride a horse the roughly twenty miles down the Colorado River to San Luis, and then even a bit farther to Mirador, Monty had decided that he was going to borrow a buckboard, two horses, and two saddles from Barney Holt's Livery. He'd ride the buckboard south, and when the killing was done, he'd pack Cain Hawker's bullet-riddled body in the buckboard and bring him back to show off to everyone in Yuma. Monty could actually visualize how impressive he would ap-

pear with the dead giant lying in the wagon. If Custis
Long survived to return with him, so much the better.
But the main thing was to bring back Cain dead for all
the world to see, and let the people of Yuma know that it
had been Monty Allison, the kid with the fast gun, who
had gotten the impossible task accomplished. And there
might even be a few dead Apaches to add to his collec-
tion and sudden fame. Hell, they might even send someone out from New York City to write a dime novel
about him, making him even more famous.

And if he failed, then so be it. As far as Monty was
concerned, he would rather go down fighting than live
with the shame that now threatened to consume him.
Shame from the fact that he had tried but failed to save
the lives of his aged and feeble parents, and allowed the
red-haired giant to humiliate and then nearly beat him to
death in his own ranch house.

The last thing that Monty did was grab his rifle and
make sure that he had four good throwing knives on his
belt. He was ready to fight, and as he eased down the
stairs and crossed the lobby, he didn't even glance at the
snoring night clerk whose head was resting on the registration desk.

Outside, he tried to keep in the shadows on Main
Street as he made his way to Holt's run-down livery
stable. Now, he realized that he really should have written a note to Mr. Holt explaining that he was just bor-
rowing the buckboard and horses for a few days. But
he'd forgotten to do that, so Mr. Holt would just have to
deal with his loss until Monty returned with a buckboard
full of dead outlaws and renegade Apache.

A short time later, Monty easily managed to catch up two good horses, and he was struggling to hitch them to the buckboard when he heard a sound behind him. Monty's hand flashed to the gun at his side, and it was up in less than a heartbeat, pointed at the silhouette of a man who'd sneaked up behind him.

"Mr. Holt? Is that you?"

"No, it's Tom Beason," the man said from the darkness as he moved closer. "You aren't going to kill me are you, kid?"

"Of course not. But I won't let you stop me from hitching up this team and helping Marshal Long down in Mirador, Mexico."

"Horse stealing is a hanging offense."

"I know that."

"It would go hard on your sister to see you hanged."

Monty took a deep breath. "I can't walk all the way out to the Double A Ranch and catch up a couple of my own horses, so I'm taking these for a few days. Don't try to stop me."

"I won't," Beason said after a long pause. "You're a stubborn one, Monty Allison."

"So I've been told."

"Since I've decided not to arrest you for horse stealing, I might as well help you hitch up that buckboard so that you can go about doing what you just have to do."

"That would be much appreciated," Monty said with genuine relief. "I sure didn't want to have to shoot you, Tom."

"I'm real happy to hear that, kid."

They got the team hitched, and just about then a

voice from the shadows cried, "Freeze! Both of you throw up your hands!"

"Don't shoot!" Tom cried. "It's me. Marshal Beason."

"Marshal Tom Beason?"

"Yeah."

"Who's the other one?"

"Monty Allison."

"Are you two stealing my buckboard and horses?"

There was silence. Then Tom finally said, "Well, of course not, Barney. We were going to wake you up and rent them."

"Oh."

"Lower that scattergun, Barney. You're making me mighty nervous."

"Well, you boys made me nervous, too! What you doing wanting to rent a buckboard and team of horses at this hour?"

"Truth of it is, Barney, we're going down to Mirador to take Cain Hawker dead or alive."

"What!" Monty said, spinning around and staring at the Yuma marshal. "You're going with me?"

"I sure as hell am," Beason heard himself say as he unpinned his badge and tossed it onto a pile of horse shit. "I am, by damned! We're both going down to Mexico because that federal marshal from Denver probably needs a hell of a lot of help."

"Well, if that isn't the craziest thing I've heard in many a day," the liveryman declared, lowering his shotgun. "And what if both you fools get shot down in Old Mexico? What am I supposed to do about losing my buckboard and a pair of my best horses?"

Tom and Monty exchanged glances, but neither could muster up a satisfactory answer.

"Well," Barney Holt said after the silence stretched thin, "I've been wanting to go down to Mirador myself for a long, long time to marry a woman named Juanita Lopez. So maybe this is as good a time as any to do 'er."

"You're coming with us?" Monty asked in disbelief.

"Why not?" Barney Holt hitched up his red nightshirt and declared, "Boys, my reason for going to Mirador to marry a pretty señorita makes a hell of a lot better sense than either of yours."

"There is going to be killing down there," Beason declared.

"I know it, and I expect to come out of it standing beside my woman in Mirador's little chapel," Holt told them. "You boys finish up there, and I'll be right back with a few more weapons and some food and whiskey."

"Whiskey will have to wait until the killin' is over," Beason advised. "Otherwise, we might be the ones that get shot all to hell."

"That's fine, Tom. Just fine with me," Barney Holt said agreeably as he hurried away to get dressed.

Tom and the kid stood in the moonlight trying to sort things out. Finally, Tom said, "Looks like there will be three of us going down to help Marshal Long."

"Looks like," Monty replied.

"Three of us and that Denver marshal . . . if he's still breathin'."

"Not too bad odds after all, is it?" Monty asked.

"Better odds than we had a right to hope for," Tom answered. "I wonder if Barney Holt can shoot a gun better than he can shovel horse shit."

Monty thought about that for almost a full minute before saying, "I strongly doubt it."

Marshal Tom Beason's hand caressed the butt of his Colt revolver. "Yeah," he said with disappointment, "I doubt it, too."

Chapter 16

Longarm awoke in the little Mexican village of Mirador late the next morning. For an instant, he blinked with surprise at his strange surroundings, and then he remembered that he was sleeping in Juanita Lopez's bed. Longarm stared up at the adobe ceiling for a moment, thinking that it was a damned good thing that the Yuma liveryman, Barney Holt, wasn't around to see this situation, or he'd be fighting mad.

Well, Longarm thought, *I've got enough fighting to do on my own right now, and this could well be my last earthly morning.*

With that thought in mind, Longarm stretched, yawned, and decided to go back to sleep.

It was almost noon when Juanita found Longarm still sawing logs. "Wake up, you lazy gringo!" she ordered, shaking Longarm by the shoulder. "Cain Hawker will be riding into town today."

Longarm sat up and rubbed the sleep from his eyes. "How do you know that?"

"Because he always comes into town on Saturday afternoon to get drunk and raise some hell in Mirador. He used to come to my cantina, but he and his men were so loud and mean that they scared off all the other customers, and I told him never to come to my cantina again."

"And he obeyed those orders?" Longarm asked with barely concealed disbelief.

"I also told him that I would kill him when he was drunk and cut off his balls with a hatchet," Juanita said with a smile. "I said that they were probably so big that I would nail them to the wall of my cantina and that would bring me many new customers from near and far."

Longarm grinned with amusement. "And that's why he doesn't drink at your place anymore?"

"That's why," Juanita said gravely. "I guess Cain didn't want his balls to be nailed to my wall for everyone to see and admire." She shrugged. "He is a huge man, but maybe he has little bitty balls like those of a ground squirrel. Eh, Marshal?"

"I have no idea and don't even want to think about it," Longarm said, sitting up and pulling on his pants while Juanita watched.

"You have big balls or you would not have come to Mirador alone," Juanita observed. "I hope that you still have them after sundown."

"Me, too."

"You want a good woman before you leave my room? She is young and pretty. I promise you will not be disappointed."

"Naw," he said, buckling on his gun belt. "I'd better keep my wits about myself and focus on what I'm going to do when Hawker and his men arrive in town. Also,

I'd better leave here without being seen so that Hawker doesn't learn that you helped me."

Juanita shrugged her bare shoulders as if it were of no concern. "Someone will have seen you last night or your animals today and asked around. Already, I would bet that all of Mirador knows that you are here hunting for Señor Hawker."

"Damn!" Longarm said with exasperation. "The only thing I had going in my favor was the element of surprise, and now you're telling me I don't even have that?"

"Maybe you do," Juanita said. "People are afraid of the red-haired demon and his bad Apache friends. They will not speak to him unless they are spoken to. Don't worry, Señor Hawker has no friends in Mirador. Not even one, although many bow and pretend that he is their good friend. But everyone is afraid of the demon and they want him dead."

"By the way. I'm curious to know how you learned to speak such good English," Longarm said.

"You think I speak very good English, huh?"

"As good as any American, and better than most."

Juanita was pleased by this compliment. "I was raised by an Irish priest in the poorest barrio in Mexico City. I grew up in his orphanage and he was a very good and godly man. When he was robbed and murdered, I ran away. Far away. I thought I would go to America to live, but I was not welcome across the border, and so I came back to this town. It was hard for many years, and then I met Barney and everything changed for me to the good."

"Barney Holt loves you," Longarm said. "Are there any men in Mirador that I could pay to stand with me?"

"No," she said. "Because they don't believe that anyone can face Cain and live to see tomorrow."

"How much time before he and the Apache are likely to ride into Mirador?" Longarm asked.

Again, the Mexican cantina owner shrugged her bare shoulders. "Who knows? Two? Maybe three hours? Maybe not even until after sundown. It is hard to say. Cain comes when he comes, and then everyone tries to disappear like rabbits down a hole."

"Well," Longarm mused, "I think I'll just find a place to hide myself and wait until he and his Apache friends are very drunk, and then I'll face them."

"Maybe they will all pass out on the dirt floor of the cantina," Juanita said hopefully. "That is often what those swine do. Or they get sick as goats on bad weeds. They are pigs, those men. Pigs that get drunk and then kill and hurt others just for the fun of it."

Longarm checked his weapons and put on his hat. "I'm leaving now. Where would you suggest that I hide?"

"If I were you, I would run north for the border so fast that I would leave that little burro in the dust."

But Longarm shook his head. "I just can't do that."

"So then maybe you should hide in the stable where your horse and your burro are being watched. From there, you can see the cantina where Cain and his friends get very drunk. If you had dynamite . . ."

"No, I won't blow them up because there will be others in the cantina."

"Only the bartender, Señor Garcia, and he would not be missed except by his mean old mother."

"No dynamite. Just tell me how to get there without being seen by the whole town."

"Go around behind my cantina and then turn right down the alley. When you come to the end of it, you will be at the back of the stable. There is a door. You can go in there and hide until it is time."

"Thank you so much, Señorita," Longarm said with heartfelt gratitude.

"If, by some miracle or the grace of God, you live through this day, will you go back to Yuma?"

"I will."

"And then you must tell Barney that Cain is dead and he should come down here to marry me before I find a big, brave man such as yourself to marry and father my children."

"I will tell him that," Longarm promised.

Juanita managed a smile, and then she kissed Longarm on the lips and stepped back. "I will pray all this day for you, Señor."

"Thank you for your prayers."

"And I will ask the priest, who is my friend, to pray for you as well and to light candles at the altar, too."

"Everything and anything that might help will be much appreciated," Longarm assured the woman.

"Adios and go with God," Juanita whispered as she left the room, leaving behind a gringo that she was almost certain would die this day.

Longarm left the room, and made his way quickly to the stable. He was relieved to see his rented horse and burro eating contentedly in separate stalls. "If I had any sense at all," he told them, "we would be leaving for Yuma within the hour."

But the horse and the burro didn't seem interested in leaving. The grass hay they were fed was rich and green.

There were a few scattered grains of corn on the floor, and the animals had both been curried to a shine.

No, the animals were plenty happy in Mirador. So happy and content that Longarm almost wished he were one of them.

Chapter 17

It was getting close to dark, and Longarm's nerves were on edge as he crouched in the stable and waited for Cain and his friends to arrive for a Saturday night of drunkenness in Mirador. He wished that he could light a cigar, but he had no matches, and the comfort of a bottle of whiskey or tequila would be the height of foolishness.

Longarm hated to spend idle time. But sometimes a man did have to wait, and there was just no help for it. Waiting was a big waste of time, and it was still hot, with many biting horseflies buzzing around in the little Mexican stable. Longarm tried to pass the time thinking about Cindy Allison, and even her cat Pedro. He had initially hoped, despite her statement to the contrary, that she might be persuaded to return with him to Colorado. After all, why would anyone want to live in the killing heat of Yuma when they could live in the high, cool air of Denver?

"But she loves it here," Longarm mused out loud. "Cindy likes the heat and she loves her ranch, and would never feel at home in a big city like Denver. And in win-

ter, when the snows blow off the eastern slopes of the
Colorado Rockies and temperatures plunge to well be-
low freezing, even I have to admit that the sunny days of
Yuma would feel mighty fine."

Longarm wondered whether, if he survived this fight,
he would still have his job back in Denver. He had left
very abruptly, and he knew that Billy Vail had not been
pleased by his sudden departure. *But yes,* Longarm
thought, *Billy will take me back with open arms.*

And so the hours passed with Longarm thinking
about all the places he'd been and the things he'd done
in his eventful and exciting life. The one thing he did not
think about was the horror and devastation of the War
Between the States. He'd had enough of that war, and
had come West in part to escape the memories.

Forever.

It was almost dusk when Longarm saw the horsemen
gallop onto the main street of the dusty Mexican village.
Cain Hawker was flanked by five short but powerful and
well-armed Apache. Longarm was almost relieved because he'd expected more Apache. Only hours before,
Juanita had brought Longarm tortillas, cold water, and a
double-barreled shotgun that had seen better days, but
which looked like it was capable of blowing a hole
through a thick stone wall.

"What gauge is this?" he'd asked the woman as he
stared at the huge muzzles and balanced the heavy old
weapon.

"I don't know. Is it big enough?"

"Yeah. It's big enough to knock a bull buffalo
flying."

"Tonight you will be shooting drunken pigs, not buffalo."

"That's right."

Juanita had kissed him one last time and left. Now, here was Cain Hawker and his Apache friends, and they were going into the cantina just as Juanita had predicted.

Longarm took a deep breath and consulted his pocket watch in the fading light. It was just a few minutes after eight o'clock. He would give his enemies three hours to get roaring drunk. Maybe even four, which would take them until midnight. Midnight sounded good to Longarm, but he sure hated the wait.

At ten fifteen by Longarm's reckoning, Cain Hawker came striding out of the cantina with his Apache, and went directly across the dusty street to barge into Juanita's cantina.

"What the hell?" Longarm muttered in confusion because he had certainly not been expecting this turn of events.

Then Longarm heard the high-pitched scream of a woman, and it sounded as if it belonged to Juanita Lopez. A moment later, Cain Hawker emerged from the cantina dragging Juanita by her long black hair. She was struggling feebly and appeared hurt.

"Marshal Custis Long!" Cain shouted across the street with a voice so loud it echoed across the surrounding hillsides. "I know you've come all the way from Denver to kill me, but I've got your lady friend and I'm going to cut her head off unless you come out of that stable unarmed!"

Longarm swore passionately. His only advantage had

suddenly been snatched away. Someone in Mirador had told the red-haired giant that Juanita was hiding the American lawman.

Cain drew a huge bowie knife from his belt and placed it next to Juanita's throat. "Come out right now with your hands reaching for heaven, or I'll be throwing her bloody head across this street and then using it for target practice!"

The five Apache were staring at the barn as if they could see right through the cracked-board wall, and Longarm knew that there was just no way to win this deadly game. He also knew that Cain wasn't bluffing.

"All right! Don't cut her throat!"

"No!" Juanita cried weakly. "He is going to kill us both anyway!"

Cain slapped her with the barrel of his gun, and there was just enough light to see fresh blood coursing down Juanita's cheek.

"All right, I'm coming out unarmed," Longarm shouted. "Don't hurt her anymore."

He had a solid-brass twin-barreled .44-caliber derringer attached to his watch fob, and now Longarm's only hope was to manage to get close enough to Cain so that he could kill the man with his deadly hideout derringer. But even if he somehow managed to kill the giant, Longarm knew that the Apache would be on him in a bloody swarm.

Longarm unbelted his cartridge belt, and was about to step into the doorway when he heard a shout of alarm and then the pounding of hoofbeats. He looked out and saw a buckboard careen around the corner on two wheels, and damned if Monty Allison, Barney Holt, and Marshal Tom Beason weren't on it with guns blazing.

Everything happened very fast after that. The Apache whirled and started shooting, but their aim was off because the buckboard was bearing down right on top of them. Two of the Apache were trampled down by the horses and wagon, and another was sent flying so hard into a horse trough that it burst and water poured into the street.

Cain Hawker had a knife in his hand instead of a gun, so he dropped the knife and went for his sidearm. Longarm had already burst from the old livery barn, and was charging the giant with his gun bucking in his big fist. Cain took one of Longarm's first bullets with no more effect than if he had been bitten by a mosquito.

Longarm's hat went sailing as Cain fired at him, and then from out of the corner of his eye Longarm saw the kid, Monty Allison, snatch a huge knife from his belt and hurl it at the giant. The knife spun in a whirling blur, and then its blade struck Cain Hawker in the side of his massive neck. A huge gusher of blood burst from the big man, and Hawker staggered backward on legs as thick as barrels. Longarm shot the giant twice, and Monty's gun was firing so rapidly that the retorts blasted down the street like the sound of unbroken rolling thunder.

Bullets were flying in all directions, and when it was over, Tom Beason was wounded in the side and Barney Holt had a crease finger-deep along his temple. But Cain Hawker and every one of the renegade Apache were either dead or dying.

Barney Holt ran to Juanita's side and cradled her in

his arms. The blood from his scalp wound dripped down on her face, but he wiped it off with his lips, and Juanita was smiling, although she was as bloody as the gringo that she loved and would soon marry.

Longarm went over to Cain Hawker, who was somehow still hanging on to life. He knelt down beside the giant and said, "Who hired you to try and kill Miss Allison and her parents at their ranch?"

Hawker was trying to pull Monty's throwing knife from out of his bull neck, but he was already too weak, so he spat bright red blood and coughed, "Go . . . to . . . Hell!"

"No," Longarm said with a shake of his head. "If there is a Hell, you're going to be there in less than one minute. So why don't you tell me who hired you to do the killing?"

Cain smiled crookedly and then hissed, "They'll hire someone else and I'll see you burning with me in Hell!"

Longarm raised his six-gun and pressed its barrel against the giant's forehead. "One last time, who hired you!"

With his face twisted in hatred, Cain tried to spit on him, and then he cursed and died.

"It's over," Tom Beason said. "We got him."

"He's dead all right, but it ain't over yet," Longarm told Yuma's town marshal. "I needed Hawker to confess who hired him. But we both already know the answer to that."

"The bankers, Caldwell and Roach."

"Yes."

"But how do you prove they were behind it?" Beason asked.

"I don't know," Longarm replied. "We'll go out to Hawker's place and see if we can find evidence tying Caldwell and Roach to the murders. Otherwise, I'll have to be creative."

"What do you mean by that?"

Longarm shrugged. "I don't know the answer to that either. But you can bet your life that I won't let those two get away with what they did to the Allison couple."

Longarm stood up and gazed around at all the carnage. The poor people of Mirador were just now starting to emerge from their hiding places, and many were pointing at Cain's body and openly smiling.

"There will be a celebration in Mirador now that the red-haired demon and his friends are dead," Juanita said loud enough for everyone. "I will donate tequila to the town and its poor people."

"Should we load Cain in the buckboard and take him back to Yuma and put him on display?" Monty Allison asked in a hopeful voice. "I sure would like to show him off so that everyone in Yuma knows that it was my favorite throwing knife and bullets that finally took him down for good."

"It's so hot that the body would corrupt by the time we arrived in Yuma."

"Not if we started out right now and traveled through the night."

"No!"

"But—"

Longarm's hand shot out and he grabbed Monty by the collar. "Listen, I sure as hell had as much to do with killing Cain Hawker as you did. Kid, trust me. You don't want to get a reputation as a killer or gunslinger, and the last thing we want to do is to make a big show of what we did down here in Old Mexico. So we'll pay these people generously to dig graves for Cain and his Apache renegades. There will be no cross, no flowers, no words from the Bible spoken over their heads. All they'll get and deserve are unmarked graves."

"Now wait a minute!" Monty protested. "There's a two-hundred-dollar reward for killing Cain Hawker and I figure it belongs to me."

"And some to me," Tom Beason said. "When all the bullets were flying, I put one on Hawker, too."

Longarm shook his head. "You know lawmen can't claim rewards. Besides, I want no part of it. All I want to do is to find enough evidence against those bankers to send them straight to the Yuma Prison for a good many years."

"Then like you said," Tom offered, "we better go to Hawker's place and see if there's any written link between him and the bankers."

Longarm heard a couple of whoops of joy from some of the barefooted peasants, and that was followed by guitar music and laughter.

"They're not waiting for tomorrow to celebrate," he said, turning full circle so he could enjoy all the happy and smiling faces.

"Juanita, are you going to help us get drunk tonight with all happy people?"

She was on her feet, being supported in Barney Holt's strong arms. "*Sí!* And tomorrow there will also be a wedding!"

"Then let the celebration begin," Longarm told her.

"Because I'm getting drunk and I'm ready to crow to the moon."

"With that young woman I offered?" Juanita asked.

Longarm thought about it for a minute. He'd passed the cantina owner up on her offer twice already, and he knew that he and Cindy Allison had no future in store, so he said, "Yeah, I'd like some female company. Does she like to drink, dance, laugh, and make good love?"

Juanita giggled. "So I'm told."

"Then we'll get acquainted and have one hell of a party!"

And with that proclamation, they left the five dead Apache and the red-haired giant and headed for Juanita's cantina, where they would spend the rest of the night.

Chapter 18

Longarm, Monty, and Tom Beason were pale and hung-over when they left Mirador late the next afternoon. They had gone to Cain Hawker's ranch and since the man was dead and had no heirs, they'd taken his horses and the few cattle that he owned. They'd also found three thousand dollars in a flour can on the kitchen shelf.

"Who gets the money?" Beason asked.

"I'll take a thousand," Longarm said. "To cover my expenses and trip back to Denver. You, Monty, and Barney Holt can split the rest."

"That and what we can split from the sale of the livestock and horses will help to pay off the loan on the ranch," Monty said. "That's all my parents ever wanted, and all Cindy wants."

"And it'll help me start over if the Yuma Town Council has fired me for leaving my job," Tom Beason added.

"I doubt that they'll fire you," Longarm told the cowboy turned lawman. "Especially when we send Caldwell and Roach to prison for hiring Cain."

"But we didn't find any proof at Cain's ranch to show that."

"Sure we did," Longarm said, patting his shirt pocket. "I have a scrap of paper in my pocket signed by both bankers with the orders to murder the Allison family."

"Where did you find that!" both Monty and Tom asked in unison.

"Doesn't matter," Longarm told them with a shrug of his shoulders.

"But . . . but if you forged the letter, then—"

"I got two separate samples of their handwriting when I was waiting to see Caldwell at the bank," Longarm said, cutting Tom off. "It's just what we need to help them confess."

Tom Beason looked closely at Longarm. "You're going to submit *forged* evidence to our circuit court judge?"

Longarm frowned and chose his next words carefully. "Tom, that's not what I said," he began. "Now, do you *really* want to continue trying to become a good lawman?"

"I think so. But Marshal Long, if you're going to perjure yourself and submit forged evidence, it makes me have second thoughts."

"Tom, in my honest opinion I don't think you're really cut out for the profession, but if you are still determined, then watch me when I go to the Bank of Yuma."

"I'll be right by your side," Tom promised.

As soon as they got to Yuma, Longarm and Tom went straight to the bank. When the teller saw them, he paled a little and then rushed into Caldwell's office. Longarm didn't wait for an invitation, and followed close on the rattled man's heels.

"What is the meaning of this interruption!" Caldwell demanded. "Marshal Beason, where have you been the last couple of days!"

"I've been in Mexico."

"Then you are fired!"

Marshal Beason's handsome but weary face darkened with anger. "Are you now the sole speaker for the Town Council?"

"You left your duty post and abandoned the citizens that you were sworn in to protect! That's inexcusable and you are fired!"

Longarm stepped in between the two men. "Mr. Caldwell, I am here to arrest you for murder."

"What!" the banker cried, almost falling out of his chair.

"You hired Cain Hawker and paid him to first kill Cindy Allison in Denver, and later to kill the rest of her family, so that you and Roach could get control of their ranch and its valuable water rights."

"You're insane!"

"Am I?" Longarm asked. "Cain Hawker confessed everything just before he died. Isn't that right, Tom?"

Tom swallowed hard, and then finally managed to nod his head.

"And," Longarm continued, "I have a written statement here by Mr. Roach saying that he opposed this arrangement and that it was all your doing!"

"What!" Caldwell shouted.

"Here it is," Longarm said, removing the forged confession from his vest and holding it up so that the banker could see it, but not too closely. "You're going to hang for those murders."

Caldwell's face went as white as chalk, and then he covered his face and wept bitterly.

"Take him to your jail and book him for murder," Longarm told the amazed Yuma marshal. "If he cooperates and gives you all the details, then maybe he'll earn a long prison sentence instead of the gallows."

Tom Beason started to say something, but his words were cut short by an anguished cry. Longarm and Beason whirled around to see the bank's assistant manager, Roach, pointing a gun at his own head. The man screamed, "I didn't want any part of hiring Cain to kill those people! It was all Raymond's fault! I'm innocent! I've done nothing! It was all his fault, not mine!"

Longarm stepped out of the manager's office, and backhanded Roach to the floor and picked up the man's gun. "Oh, you're responsible, too. And you'll go to prison just like he will."

Assistant Manager Roach covered his face and sobbed uncontrollably. Longarm dragged him to his feet and marched him toward the door and jail.

"Put 'em in separate rooms until you get a full written statement that may or may not save them from the hangman's noose," he told Beason.

"Yes, sir!"

Longarm heard the train whistle blow, and he knew that the train would be leaving in less than an hour, which was just enough time to grab his belongings from the Rawhide Hotel and be on his way out of this godforsaken desert.

"Custis!"

He stopped in the street and saw Cindy rushing toward him. They embraced, and then Longarm led her silently up to his hotel room.

"I'm leaving today on that train," he said quietly.

"But can't you stay just awhile!"

"No. I had a woman down in Mirador. It's over between us, Cindy. Your future is here and mine is back in Denver. With my job and with your cat."

Tears filled her eyes. "You took a woman down in Mexico?"

"I did," he said, hating himself. "Because I knew that doing so would make our parting final."

She was crying softly. "But . . . but I was thinking about going back with you!"

"You'd never be happy, and I'd never be a good mate or husband for you, Cindy. It would never have worked out."

Longarm expelled a deep breath. "Look," he told her quietly. "With the reward and the money that Monty earned down in Mexico and with Tom Beason's money, you can pay off the bank and restock the Double A with cattle. Your Double A Ranch can prosper again, Cindy. You'll be able to have a good life here in Arizona."

"I . . . I don't see what Tom's money has to do with anything."

"That's because you don't realize that the man is hopelessly in love with you and you're destined to marry him."

Cindy's blue eyes widened. "I am?"

"Yes. Tom has more than proven he's a good man, but not cut out to be a town marshal. Make him hand in his badge before he gets killed. Marry him and he'll make you happy and he can go back to being a cowboy and rancher again. That's his real destiny."

Cindy dried her tears and squared her strong shoulders. "You seem to be pretty good at telling other people what their destinies are. Are you so very sure you even know your own?"

"I do," Longarm said, lips brushing her wet cheek in a final good-bye, "and I'd already found it when we met that morning on Colfax Avenue in Denver."

She managed a smile and raised her head high. "I . . . I see."

"Cindy, I'm very happy that you do," Longarm told her as he picked up his bag and headed downstairs to catch his train.

Watch for

LONGARM AND THE SHOTGUN MAN

the 370th novel in the exciting LONGARM
series from Jove

Coming in September!

GIANT-SIZED ADVENTURE FROM
AVENGING ANGEL LONGARM.

BY TABOR EVANS

penguin.com/actionwesterns

M456AS0409

DON'T MISS A YEAR OF

Slocum Giant
by
Jake Logan

Slocum Giant 2004:
Slocum in the Secret Service

Slocum Giant 2005:
Slocum and the Larcenous Lady

Slocum Giant 2006:
Slocum and the Hanging Horse

Slocum Giant 2007:
Slocum and the Celestial Bones

Slocum Giant 2008:
Slocum and the Town Killers